Kristy's Worst Idea

Other books by
Ann M. Martin

Kristy's Worst Idea

Ann M. Martin

AN
APPLE
PAPERBACK

SCHOLASTIC INC.
New York Toronto London Auckland Sydney

Cover art by Hodges Soileau

ISBN 0-590-69206-2

12 11 10 9 8 7 6 5 4 3 2 1   6 7 8 9/9 0 1/0

Printed in the U.S.A.   40

First Scholastic printing, September 1996

*The author gratefully acknowledges
Peter Lerangis
for his help in
preparing this manuscript.*

CHAPTER 1

"Sorry, Mary Anne, I can't hear you!" I shouted into the phone receiver.

Mary Anne Spier cleared her throat and began, "I *said*, hi, I really missed you, and — "

"EEEEEEEE!" That was my two-year-old sister, Emily Michelle, racing through the kitchen.

Behind her was my youngest brother, David Michael (seven, going on three). He was brandishing an ugly figurine carved from a coconut, which he'd somehow convinced my mom and dad to buy in Hawaii. "Nyyyah-hah-hah, the coco-monster's going to get you!"

I stepped out of his way. My foot hooked into a backpack that was on the floor, and I fell into a kitchen chair.

"ANYBODY SEEN MY BACKPACK?" called my seventeen-year-old brother, Charlie, from upstairs.

"UNDER MY FEET!" I shouted back.

1

"WHERE ARE YOUR FEET?"

"IN THE KITCHEN!"

The Thomas/Brewer family was in total, utter chaos.

It was 11:00 A.M. on the Sunday before Labor Day. My family was just waking up, groggy and jetlagged. We'd arrived in the wee hours of the morning from a vacation in sunny, exciting, beach-filled Hawaii. (I had a fantastic time, thanks for asking.) Our flight back had taken almost a whole day. That part wasn't so great.

You see, we'd left Hawaii on Saturday at eight A.M. We landed in Los Angeles five hours later, but our connecting flight was delayed for four hours. Well, L.A. time is two hours later than Hawaii time, so it was dinner hour when we boarded the next plane for another five-hour flight that actually put us in New York eight hours later, because of the three-hour time change. Then, after waiting forty-five minutes for our luggage, we took an hour-and-a-half limo ride from New York to Stoneybrook, Connecticut.

Got all that? Okay, for the grand prize, what time was it when we walked into our house?

(Don't expect me to know. I was fast asleep.)

When I'd finally staggered downstairs on Sunday morning, I'd found three messages from Mary Anne on the answering machine. Message one was a cheerful "Call me when you're home." Message two sounded a little concerned.

By message three, I could tell she was fighting back tears. Thinking we were kidnapped. Imagining we'd decided to move to Hawaii. (Actually, that doesn't sound like a bad idea. . . .)

Mary Anne is a real worrywart. Not to mention shynesswart and politenesswart. The teeniest things can make her cry, too — movies, books, you name it. Whisper the words "Old Yeller" to her and watch her eyes well up. Usually I have no patience for people like that. I'm the opposite — tearless and fearless, loud and proud. But I've known Mary Anne since we were babies, and she happens to be my best friend in the world.

As you may have guessed, I have a forceful personality. My friends say I'm bossy and stubborn, but don't listen to them. They're all members of the Baby-sitters Club (more about that later), and I'm their president, so bossiness is just part of the deal. Period.

Here are the other vital facts about me: I'm thirteen years old and just barely five feet tall. I have brown hair and brown eyes, and I'm very athletic. I wear casual clothes all the time, and I think fashion is boring.

Okay. Enough about me. Back to Mary Anne.

I was dying to talk to her. Half of me wanted to ask how the club had survived. The other half wanted to gab about Hawaii. Mary Anne had been there on a school trip in July, along with almost all of my other BSC (Baby-sitters Club) friends.

"Sorry about the noise, Mary Anne," I shouted into the phone as Emily Michelle zipped by. *"Emily, go to Nannie!"*

"I'm glad you're home," Mary Anne replied. "I have been soooo lonely, and — "

"I'm starving!" announced my middle brother, Sam, stomping toward the kitchen. "Yo, Blabberlips, when are you going to be off the phone?"

Sam's fifteen, but sometimes he has the maturity of a toddler. (Why am I the only Thomas kid who acts her age?) Ignoring his obnoxious comment, I pressed the receiver to my ear and tried to listen.

"House of Wiley?" asked Mary Anne. (That's what it sounded like. It was hard to tell over the noise.)

"Whaaat?" I asked.

Sam rolled his eyes. "I *said*, when are you going to be off the phone?"

"How . . . was . . . Hawaii?" Mary Anne said loudly.

4

Before I could answer either of them, Sam pulled open the fridge, releasing a blast of putrid air. I nearly gagged.

"Yeccch, it stinks!" I blurted out.

"Really?" Mary Anne said. "I think it's magical."

"No, not Hawaii! Our fridge!"

Sam slammed the door shut. "What died in there?"

"*Someone died?*" Mary Anne asked.

I held my nose. "Doe! Just sub boldy food."

(Take some advice from me, Kristy Thomas. If you're going on vacation, don't ever leave an open bowl of tuna salad in your fridge.)

Charlie clomped into the kitchen and glared at me. "Talk fast. I want to call Sarah." (That's his girlfriend.)

"Hey, me first!" Sam insisted.

"Who are *you* calling?" Charlie demanded.

"None of your business!" Sam snapped.

"Uh, Kristy," Mary Anne asked patiently, "is this a bad time to talk?"

"Nope." I walked toward the kitchen archway, away from the stench and the argument. "Mary Anne, I actually tried to surf. You should have seen me. You will die when I show you the pictures."

Charlie and Sam were arguing at the top of their lungs. Nannie was chasing after Emily

Michelle with a change of clothes. David Michael came in and pretended to faint from the smell. Mom bustled in and yelled at Charlie and Sam for not cleaning the fridge.

"Guys, will you please be quiet?" I yelled.

Honestly, you'd think it would be easy to find peace and quiet in a mansion. But nooooo. Everyone just had to be in the same room as Kristy.

Yes, you heard right. Mansion. With fancy wallpaper, high ceilings, lots of wood trim everywhere, and a big yard. Cool, huh?

Don't think I'm a rich snob or anything. I'm casual, down-to-earth, and friendly as can be. (Modest, too. Heh heh.) Actually, I was not born into wealth. I grew up in a small house across town, next door to Mary Anne. My mom raised Charlie, Sam, David Michael, and me while holding a full-time job (my dad ran off soon after David Michael was born).

Things became easier after Mom married Watson. For one thing, he's a nice guy who doesn't abandon his loved ones (ahem). For another, we live in this house that looks like something out of *Lifestyles of the Rich and Famous*.

Well, maybe *Lifestyles of the Crowded and Noisy*. And only part of our family was in the house that Sunday. Our family, as you can see, has expanded since Mom's remarriage.

6

Emily Michelle is the youngest member. She was born in Vietnam and adopted by Watson and Mom, which I guess makes her the only full-fledged Brewer/Thomas. Nannie is our oldest member. She's my grandmother, and she moved in to help take care of Emily Michelle. Watson has two children from his first marriage, Karen (who's seven) and Andrew (four), who live with us during alternate months.

(Remind me to tell you about our hermit crab, cat, goldfish, rat, and puppy. They're part of the family, too.)

Pulling the phone cord as far as it could go, I stood just outside the kitchen.

Watson was walking toward the kitchen now, his face slowly turning green. "Uh, Elizabeth?" he said to Mom. "I'll be happy to go and buy some breakfast food if you clean that thing out."

"I'll go with you!" Charlie and Sam shouted at the same time.

"One of you stays with me!" Mom said, pulling Sam back by the shirttail.

"Mo-*ommmm*," Sam groaned (served him right).

I covered up the receiver and called after Charlie, "Pick up Sarah on your way to the store. You can wheel the cart down the aisle together like lovebirds."

Charlie yanked open the fridge and ran out the front door, laughing.

I wanted to kill him.

"EWWWW!" I shouted.

"EWWWW!" shrieked Emily Michelle, running through the kitchen again.

"EWWWW!" echoed David Michael.

Mom put on her yellow latex gloves, ready to do Odor Battle.

"I'll go pick up another extension," I whispered to Mary Anne.

Mom gave me her *don't-think-you-can-get-out-of-this-one* look. "Kristyyyy . . ."

Too late. I absolutely shattered the record for the cross-house dash and dove for the phone in the family room. "I'm here," I said, picking up the receiver. "Tell me how much everyone in the BSC missed me, in fifty words or less."

Mary Anne laughed. "A lot, Kristy. But we survived. Abby really improved as president."

I should have been happy to hear that. Thrilled. I mean, I care about the Baby-sitters Club more than anything else. But somehow that statement made me feel as if I'd swallowed a rotting turnip. Don't get me wrong. I like Abby Stevenson, but she'd been really snide to me during a meeting I'd let her run in August.

"Great," I said.

"She finally realized that cutting the dues was a bad idea — "

"I hate to tell you I told her that," I said. "But I told her that."

"Well, see, we needed money for the Mexican festival." (That was this big fair she organized to raise money for a Mexican orphanage.)

"The festival turned out to be really fun," Mary Anne added.

"Uh-huh," I replied. "Fantastic."

I was stoic. Upbeat. Positive. But inside, the turnip was putrefying.

"Is everything okay, Kristy?" (Leave it to Mary Anne. She absolutely reads my mind.)

"Fine, fine."

"RRRAAAAAGH!" David Michael sprang up from the side of the sofa with his toy monster, nearly scaring me to death.

"Can't you see I'm on the phone?" I blurted out.

"Hey, why is *she* allowed to loaf around?" Sam complained from the kitchen.

"Listen, Mary Anne," I said, "it's just crazy around here. Maybe I can bike over later — "

"Don't make plans, Kristy!" Mom called out. "We have a full two days ahead — picking up Shannon from the kennel, school shopping, unpacking, putting the house back together . . ."

"Mom's on the warpath," I whispered into the phone. "We'll talk at the meeting tomorrow, okay?"

"Meeting?" Mary Anne said.

"Tomorrow's Monday, right?"

"Well, yeah. But it's Labor Day."

"So? The BSC's not *labor*," I pointed out.

"I know, but it is a holiday, and I don't think any clients will be calling, and besides — "

"Even better. We'll need a quiet meeting before the school year starts. We can update our records, talk about the summer, make plans for the year. Anyway, we have to meet because I brought you all presents!"

"Well . . . okay," Mary Anne said softly. "But I know Jessi's family is having a big barbecue, and I think Claudia was supposed to go to her aunt's house — "

"Don't worry, I'll call them," I said. "Got to go. Can't wait to see you!"

I hung up and raced into the battle zone.

Despite the smells and noise, I was suddenly feeling great.

Okay, I wasn't in Waikiki. I wasn't watching the sun rise over the rim of an ancient volcano.

But I was home. And in a day, I'd be running a Baby-sitters Club meeting.

As far as I was concerned, life couldn't be much better than that.

Claudia Kishi gasped as she opened the present I'd bought her. "Kristy, I don't know what to say."

For all to see, she held up a huge pineapple-shaped clock, whose two hands were a surfer and a surfboard.

"How about, 'That's the ugliest thing I have ever seen'?" Abby suggested.

Claudia, Abby, Stacey McGill, and Mallory Pike all howled with laughter. (Mary Anne chuckled politely.)

Abby was wearing her hula-grass hat. Stacey was strumming her toy ukelele. Mary Anne's mirrored sunglasses were reflecting the light in Claudia's bedroom. Mallory was trying on her pink-and-blue lei-shaped clip-on earrings.

Claudia's clock clicked to 5:30. I cleared my throat and announced, "I hereby call to order the first Baby-sitters Club Luau!"

Splink.

That was Stacey, trying to play a tune on her ukelele.

"Anyone know where Jessi is?" I asked.

"Her parents wouldn't let her leave the barbecue," Mallory piped up.

"Smart people," mumbled a voice in the hallway.

Claudia spun around. "Who asked you?"

Claudia's older sister, Janine, poked her head in the door. "Well, they *are*. The last time I looked, this day was a federal holiday."

With that, she disappeared down the hall and into her bedroom.

"She's sour because we had to come home early from Peaches' and Russ's party," Claudia said with a shrug. "Russ had just put the duck on the grill."

"*Duck?*" Stacey said.

Abby nodded solemnly. "I've had that. We call it barbequack."

"Uh, Kristy?" Mallory began. "My mom wanted to know if we could end a little early today. My uncle Joe is visiting from the nursing home, and he never likes to stay too long."

Claudia's eyes lit up. "Oooh, great idea. Maybe we can all go back to the barbequack."

"Whoa, first things first," I reminded everyone. "Any new business?"

"Dues day!" Stacey reached under Claudia's

12

bed and pulled out a manila envelope.

The air filled with groans.

"On a holiday?" Abby asked.

I raised an eyebrow. "After what happened this summer, I don't think we can afford to skip any dues."

"Well, excuuuuse me!" Abby murmured.

I know, I know, I was being a little harsh. But hey, someone has to lay down the law. The Baby-sitters Club is all about balance — keeping fun and business in the right proportions.

I should know. I invented the BSC. Well, that's not totally true. Kristy's Law, Part One: Great ideas invent themselves. You see, back in the days before Watson, I watched Mom spend one entire afternoon trying to line up a baby-sitter for David Michael. She must have made a hundred phone calls. What she needed was obvious: a group of sitters, available at one central number.

All I did was provide it.

First I recruited Claudia, Mary Anne, and Stacey. Since Claud has her own private phone line, we decided to use her room as a meeting place. We established regular hours (Mondays, Wednesdays, and Fridays from five-thirty to six) and advertised all over town.

Parents could now call one number and reach four available sitters. (I mean, *duh*, right?

I couldn't believe no one had thought of it before.)

Kristy's Law, Part Two: Great ideas grow like wildfire. It sure happened to us. Now we have seven regular members, two associates, and one honorary member. We have a ton of regular clients, and we're always busy. Often we organize special events for our charges. How do we do it all? Smoothly. You see, I made sure we had a tight structure: officers with specific duties, a treasury, a record book containing a job calendar and client list, and a notebook with personal remarks about each baby-sitting experience.

I'm president. I call the meetings to order and make sure we take care of business.

As secretary, Mary Anne has the hardest job. She's in charge of the record book. She lists all of our jobs on the calendar, along with our conflicts — lessons, family trips, doctor appointments. When a parent calls, Mary Anne can see exactly who's available, and she tries to distribute jobs evenly among us. On top of that, she's constantly updating the client list, which contains rates, addresses, phone numbers, emergency contacts, birthdays, and special information about our charges.

I may think of the big ideas, but Mary Anne puts them into action (maybe that's why we're such good friends). She could organize the hay

14

in a haystack into size groupings. That part of her personality comes from her dad, Richard. (Maybe the sweetness and shyness came from her mom, but we'll never know. Mrs. Spier died when Mary Anne was a baby.) Richard raised Mary Anne strictly. Right through seventh grade, Mary Anne had to wear her hair in pigtails, go to bed super early, and wear little-girl clothes.

Don't worry. Richard reformed before things became too embarrassing. Mary Anne's life has changed a lot. Nowadays she wears normal clothes and a cool, short hairstyle. She also has a steady boyfriend named Logan Bruno, who's an associate BSC member. Not only that, but the Spier family has grown from two to five. That's because Richard met his high school sweetheart again after a gazillion years, and they fell head over heels in love and married.

That sweetheart just happened to be the divorced mom of another BSC member, Dawn Schafer. Where had the love of Richard's life been all these years? In California, raising Dawn and her brother, Jeff. After her divorce, she moved with Dawn and Jeff into this funky two-hundred-year-old Stoneybrook farmhouse. When Dawn moved to Stoneybrook, she and Mary Anne discovered the love secret and reintroduced their parents. Soon they went from being good friends to being stepsisters! (Dawn and Jeff both came down with severe California-homesickness, though. In time, each of them moved back to live with their dad.)

Dawn had been our alternate officer, the person who takes over the job of any officer who's absent. When she moved, we tried to manage without taking in a new member. Fat chance. We were totally swamped. I was on the verge of a nervous breakdown. Then — ta-da! — Abby Stevenson moved into town from Long Island. We quickly invited her to join the club, and she accepted.

Now I'm having that nervous breakdown.

Just kidding. Abby's great. She's the most gung-ho athlete in the BSC besides me, despite the fact it takes her an hour to arm-wrestle her thick, curly hair into a ponytail whenever she plays sports. Really, you have to see her do that. She turns it into a comedy act. In fact, she turns a lot of things into a comedy act (including the BSC presidency, I guess). If you ever meet her, don't be surprised if she sounds as if she has a cold. She's allergic to a thousand different things. On top of that, she's an asthmatic and always carries inhalers with her. Her attacks are scary but controllable. She likes to remind everyone that Teddy Roosevelt had asthma. (He, however, was a much better president.)

Abby and her twin sister, Anna, live two houses away from mine. Their mom is a book editor and commutes to a New York City publishing company every day. (Mr. Stevenson died when the girls were nine or so, but they don't talk about him often, so I don't know much about him.)

Anna and Abby are sort of like Mary Anne and me — total opposites. Anna's sweet, kind, thoughtful, and not interested in sports. Her great passion is the violin, which she practices constantly. (Ask me to hum the Mendelssohn Violin Concerto. In fact, ask the whole neighborhood. We heard it about three million times during July, when Anna was learning parts of it for a recital.) To be honest, I was hoping Anna would join the BSC, too, but she declined the offer.

The Stevensons are Jewish, and recently the twins became Bat Mitzvahs. All of us BSC members went to the ceremony, which is kind of a religious growing-up ritual for thirteen-year-old girls. It's a great idea, if you ask me, even though you have to recite a lot of stuff in Hebrew.

Between Abby and Claudia, our BSC meetings sometimes become half-hour-long laff riots. Their senses of humor are different, though. Claudia's not really a comedian, like Abby. She just has the world's oddest way of looking at life. To her, the most ordinary thing is an object of art. For instance, at that Labor Day meeting she was wearing a bracelet of dyed, braided shoelaces, along with a blousy ruffled shirt that looked as if it once belonged to Captain Hook; mismatched high-top Converse sneakers; and baggy, pinstriped men's suit pants, gathered at the waist with a bungee cord. On me, something like that would look like a Halloween costume. On Claudia it looked way cool.

Everything she touches — not just her outfits — turns into a work of art. She's a fantastic sculptor, painter, sketcher, and jewelry maker. I have no idea who she gets that talent from. The others in her family are brainy types. Especially Janine, whose IQ looks like a world-record bowling score. Mr. and Mrs. Kishi appreciate Claudia's artistic talent, but you can tell they also wish she were a better student.

The Kishis, in my opinion, need to loosen up. They forbid junk food, insist on rigid homework hours, and won't even allow Claudia to read Nancy Drew books because they're too "commercial." (Claudia's addicted to them, so she has to hide the ones she buys.)

Claudia's also addicted to junk food, which

she hides right alongside her books. Honestly, Claudia sucks down chocolate and yet she is totally zitless and slim. She's gorgeous, too, with silky black hair and a smooth, creamy complexion (she's Japanese-American).

By the way, Claudia is our vice-president. Her main functions are official host, junk-food caterer, and answerer of the phone during off-hours.

She passed around a bag of caramel corn while Stacey counted out our dues money.

"Heyyy, good news," Stacey announced. "After we pay Claudia's phone bill for the month, we'll have . . . uh, a positive amount in the treasury."

"How positive?" I asked.

"Three dollars and seventeen cents," Stacey replied with a sheepish smile.

That wasn't what I'd expected to hear. *"Three dollars —* " I blurted out.

"Let's celebrate!" Claudia exclaimed, jumping off her bed. She disappeared into the closet and returned with a tiny gumball machine in the shape of a dolphin. "Is this cute or what?"

"Wait a minute," I began. "We should have much more than — "

"Unforeseen expenses," Abby quickly piped up.

Claudia started tossing gumballs around the room. "You drop it, you lose it."

(Honestly, they walk all over me sometimes.)

As Abby waited her turn, she clapped her hands and barked like a seal. The gumball smacked against one of her front teeth, and her seal imitation suddenly sounded like a wounded pup.

Stacey waved Claudia off. "No, thanks."

"Don't worry, they're sugarless," Claudia said.

No, Stacey is not a weight-watcher. She's diabetic. Her body doesn't make this hormone called insulin (which is sort of a valet parking service for sugar molecules: it stores them for awhile, then lets them out over time into the bloodstream). Too much sugar, and Stacey could become seriously ill, and lose consciousness. But she's able to lead a normal life with a strict, regular diet, and daily injections of insulin. (I've seen her do it, and it's not as gross as it sounds.)

What does a diabetic look like? Well, if she's anything like Stacey McGill, stunning. You could easily mistake her for sixteen. She has long, golden-blonde hair, and she dresses like a model. She says she picked up her fashion sense just by observing people in New York City, where she grew up. (I don't know who she observed, because whenever I go there I see a lot of people in jeans and T-shirts.) Stacey still visits the Big Apple a lot. Her parents are divorced, and her dad lives in an apartment there.

Stacey is our treasurer, mainly because she's the only BSC member who actually likes math. She collects dues every Monday. Here's what we do with the money, besides contributing to Claudia's phone bill: We reimburse my brother Charlie for his gas expenses when he drives me and Abby to meetings. We buy supplies for Kid-Kits, which are boxes of toys and games we sometimes take to our jobs. We organize fund-raisers for our school and for charities. We put together field days and parties for our charges. And once in awhile we treat ourselves to a pizza party. As you can see, running a good club is not cheap.

Which is why Stacey should never, *never* have let Abby mess around with the dues.

Ahem.

Okay, okay. Enough on that topic. It's the last time I'll bring it up. Promise.

Back to the BSC. Our other regular members are Jessica Ramsey and Mallory Pike. We call them our junior officers because they're eleven years old and in sixth grade. (The rest of us are thirteen and in eighth.) Their parents don't allow them to take nighttime sitting jobs unless they're taking care of their own siblings, but they take plenty of jobs in the afternoon.

Jessi and Mal are absolute best friends. They're both the oldest kid in their families, and they love to complain that their parents treat them like babies. They're also major horse fanatics. Show them any *Black Beauty* or *Saddle Club* book ever written, and they'll tell you the plot in more detail than you'll want to know.

They're not total clones, though. Jessi's African-American and Mallory's Caucasian. Jessi's a phenomenal ballet dancer, and Mal likes to write and illustrate her own stories. Jessi has two younger siblings and Mal has seven, including ten-year-old triplet brothers (if you can imagine such a horror).

Our two associate members help us out when we're super busy, but they aren't required to attend meetings or pay dues. One of them is Mary Anne's steady boyfriend, Logan Bruno. He's kind of cute, if you like the dimply, dirty-blond, athletic type, and he speaks with a slight Kentucky accent. Our other associate is Shannon Kilbourne, who lives in my neighborhood and goes to a private school called Stoneybrook Day School. Shannon has curly blonde hair and a bubbly personality, and she's a real joiner — honor society, drama club, chorus, Spanish club, you name it.

Dawn Schafer is our honorary member.

Now that she lives in California, though, she belongs to a different baby-sitting group called the We ♥ Kids Club (a kind of sloppy, unprofessional imitation of the BSC — but they're nice girls).

"Any other business?" I called out.

Stacey nodded. "My father bought me a ticket to a Broadway show for Friday night and he wants to have dinner beforehand."

Abby put her hands to her cheeks, like Macaulay Culkin in *Home Alone*. "Doesn't he know it's the night of a BSC meeting?"

"Can he exchange it?" I asked.

"I was joking, Kristy," Abby said.

Stacey gave me a Look. "You can't exchange Broadway tickets. I just wanted to let you know I won't be here."

Mallory's hand shot up. "As long as we're talking about Friday, Jessi told me to tell you that her new ballet class meets Fridays at five-fifteen."

"Every Friday?" I asked. "Is that the only class she can take?"

Mallory nodded. "It's level three, only one class per week. Jessi begged Mme Noelle to change the time. A few other kids didn't like it, either."

"We could have our meetings at the dance studio," Abby suggested.

"And feed the ballerinas junk food," Claudia added.

"Welcome to *Swine Lake*," Abby said in an announcer's voice.

"Whoa, guys, this is serious," I said. "The year hasn't even started and everyone's ducking out."

"Well, Jessi suggested we change the Friday meetings to Thursdays," Mallory went on. "You know, permanently."

"No way!" I blurted out. "Our meeting days are, like, stamped in our clients' brains."

Abby rolled her eyes. "Oh, Kristy, come on. They can take it. They're parents. They're used to changing schedules."

"Out of the question," I insisted.

"Why?" asked Stacey.

I shook my head. "I don't believe we're even talking about this. First of all, think of Claudia. She'll be answering the phone a million times on Friday for the parents who forget."

"No big deal," Claudia said with a shrug. "I can always turn on the answering machine if I'm in the middle of a super-interesting spelling assignment."

Everyone started laughing, but I barged right on. "That's another thing. Why are Friday meetings such fun? Because it's not a homework night. Thursday *is*."

"Yeah, but parents go out Friday nights,"

Stacey pointed out. "They'd probably prefer us to meet on Thursdays."

"We could survey them," Mallory suggested.

"It won't work," I said. "Trust me. Besides, we've always scheduled personal stuff around Fridays. I'll bet our Thursdays are full of conflicts already."

Mary Anne, who had been silent, was leafing through the record book. "Actually, they're pretty clear."

"Well, they won't be for long," I replied.

"So Jessi has to quit ballet?" Mallory asked.

I shrugged. "Or the BSC."

"Oh, come *on*, that's unfair," Abby protested.

"We could just try Thursday meetings for awhile, Kristy," Mary Anne said. "Or excuse Jessi from Fridays."

"Let's vote," Abby announced. "All in favor of Thursdays say 'Cheese.' "

"*Cheeeeeese!*" cried everyone but me and Mary Anne.

"All opposed say 'Crackers,' " Abby went on.

"Uh, excuse me," I said. "Did I miss something? I thought *I* was the president, and you were my temporary replacement."

Abby bowed her head low. "Sorry, my liege."

They were all giggling like monkeys.

"Very funny," I snapped. "Did you *all* stop taking this club seriously while I was gone, or just Abby?"

"Kristy, all she did was ask for a vote," Claudia said.

"We *were* serious this summer," Abby added. "The Mexican festival wasn't exactly a day at the beach."

"We raised a lot of money," Stacey added.

"You would have been proud," Mal spoke up.

Proud of Abby's idea? Right. Look what it had done. The whole club had been Abbified. Everyone had grown lazy while I was gone.

Or maybe they weren't lazy. Maybe I was being too stubborn. (Hard to imagine, I know.) Sometimes you have to give a little to keep people happy.

I realized it was time to snap back. Win everyone back to my side. I had to come up with an idea of my own. A fantastic project to kick off the new school year.

"Okay, Thursday meetings," I relented. "Now let's move on to something new. The Fall Into Fall Festival Block Party."

"The who?" Claudia asked.

Good question. I wasn't sure myself yet. The words had just flown out of my mouth. I barreled on anyway. "Look, the summer's over. Families are returning to Stoneybrook. Some of the parents haven't seen us since the spring. What's on their minds? School supplies, classroom numbers, clothing, groceries. Well, we have to add one more ingredient to that list — and you know what it is, guys."

Claudia nodded sagely. "Ring-Dings. They go great in lunch boxes."

"No!" I snapped. "The Baby-sitters Club. That's where the Fall Into Fall Festival Block Party comes in. We'll close off McLelland Road on a Saturday. Advertise all over town. Have the best fall activities. Apple picking, cider making, maple sugaring — "

"Maple sugaring?" Abby asked.

"Apple picking?" Stacey piped up. "Who has an apple tree?"

"It's simple — " I began.

Rrrrring!

Claudia snatched up the phone. "Hello, Baby-sitters Club! Oh, hi, Mrs. DeWitt. Thursday after school? Well, we're pretty free at this point. But let me call you back."

Mary Anne was running her finger down the September calendar. Claudia, Abby, and Stacey were looking at me as if I had gone off my rocker. Mallory was waiting to hear the rest of my plan.

It was taking shape right in my little brain. Growing. Turning into a real Kristy Thomas winner.

Forget about the Mexican festival. This was going to be the event of the century.

CHAPTER 3

Wednesday

Claudia and me.
Barrett/DeWitts. Kids
difficult. Nervous
about the school year.
Played games.
Art, too.

No, Mary Anne and Claudia were not studying shorthand. They were in bad moods.

At first I hadn't really noticed. I mean, the whole room felt kind of toxic during our Wednesday meeting.

Abby was still sore at me for what I'd said on Monday. Stacey was worrying about some social studies research project. Jessi apologized every other minute for her ballet conflict. Mary Anne spent practically the whole meeting hunched over the record book, with her hair in front of her face. Mallory was busy comforting Jessi. And Claudia was staring out her window, munching on Doritos.

Me? I was no bag of chuckles myself.

Things did not improve on Thursday. If anything, they became worse. Boy, was it strange meeting on two consecutive days. I kept thinking it was Friday and I wouldn't have school the next day. But noooo. What was worse, we received zero calls.

Why? Beats me. Our clients must have known about our schedule change. We'd spent most of the week calling everyone we could. We'd also put up fliers around town that looked like this:

Attention All Parents!
*** *Bulletin!!!* * * *
The Baby-Sitters Club Announces
Its New, Improved Schedule:
Monday, Wednesday, and
Thursday
5:30 to 6:00
Same Great Service —
more Convenient Hours!

Maybe no one had gone into town during the week.

Oh, well. We all sort of moped through the meeting and went home.

That evening I called Mary Anne. I figured talking to her would cheer me up.

I had no idea what she'd been through on Wednesday at the Barrett/DeWitts. She filled me in on every gory detail.

The job had started out okay. She and Claudia had walked to their job from school, complaining about schoolwork and the normal beginning-of-the-year stuff.

Mrs. DeWitt met them at the door. She was smiling, but her eyes had that *get-me-out-of-here* look. "So glad you could come," she said. "Buddy's having a time-out in the basement, Lindsey's having a time-out upstairs in her bedroom, Taylor and Suzi are not allowed to watch any TV, and all of them

31

have lost their cookie privileges until tomorrow. Ryan's eating a snack in the high chair. Marnie and Madeleine are probably hungry, too. The time-out buzzer will go off any minute. I should be back around five-fifteen. 'Bye.''

Zoom. She was out of the house.

Claud and Mary Anne just stood there, nodding.

On a normal day, the Barrett/DeWitts are a pretty wild bunch — seven kids from two different marriages. When Mrs. DeWitt is in a mood like that, you wish you'd brought along protective armor.

As the front door closed, Mary Anne heard Buddy's voice scream out, "MO-O-O-OM! CAN I COME UP NOW?"

"Dess-ee! Dess-ee!" cried two-year-old Marnie as she charged into the front room. When she saw Mary Anne and Claudia, her face fell. "No Dess-ee?"

(Translation: Jessi. Marnie has a huge crush on her these days.)

Four-year-old Madeleine DeWitt stomped in, all pouty-looking. "That's not Jessi, you silly face!"

"Where Dess-ee?" Marnie asked.

Madeleine glared at her. "Jessi's dead!"

"Madeleine!" Mary Anne blurted out.

"Jessi's dead, Miss Raymond's dead, my

whole school is dead, *I'm* dead!" Madeleine shouted, stalking away.

Marnie's lips were quivering. Her face was turning bright red. She let out a high-pitched wail.

Mary Anne scooped her up. "Shhh, Madeleine doesn't mean that."

"Lindsey hit me!" Suzi Barrett cried, running into the room. "And she left her bedroom, even though she's having a time-out." (Suzi, by the way, is five. Lindsey DeWitt and Buddy Barrett are both eight.)

"You made me!" yelled Lindsey from upstairs. "You were teasing me from the hallway!"

"MO-O-O-OM! IS MY TIME-OUT OVER?" Buddy's voice boomed.

DZZZZZZZZZZ! erupted the kitchen stove buzzer.

Thump-thump-thump-thump went two sets of stairs as Buddy rushed up and Lindsey rushed down.

"Waaaah!" cried Marnie, still upset over Jessi's untimely demise.

CRASH!

That was a plastic plate Ryan had dropped in the kitchen. (He's two years old, too.)

"Eeeeew!" shouted Buddy and Lindsey, running into the family room.

Claudia and Mary Anne raced into the kitchen. Six-year-old Taylor DeWitt was busy smearing applesauce and cut-up bananas into the kitchen tile with a dish towel. "I'm cleaning up!"

"Uh, let me help you," Claudia volunteered, running for a sponge.

"My teacher's name is Jody," Taylor announced. "Her last name is Andrews. On the first day of school, she made us tell about our summers."

Claudia knelt down and started sponging up the mess. "That's nice."

"More 'nanas," Ryan demanded.

"This kid, David?" Taylor plunged on. "He went to New Hampshire, I think. And Ripley? He took tae kwon do, but when he showed us a kick the teacher got mad. And Annie? She lives on our street?"

"Will you stop?" Lindsey shouted from the family room. "We heard this a million times!"

"My teacher's name is Mrs. Pimpleface," Buddy said in a singsong voice, "and I'm going to poison her."

"Don't talk about schoooool!" Lindsey screamed.

"Yeah!" Madeleine agreed from her corner of the room.

Mary Anne set Marnie down and ducked into the family room. There, Buddy was furiously playing a Game Boy. Lindsey was staring glumly out the window and Madeleine was curled up in an armchair, spinning the wheels of a toy train.

"What's up, you guys?" Mary Anne asked, sitting on the sofa. "School getting you down already?"

No answer.

"Pow!" Buddy said, punching the buttons of his Game Boy. "I'm blowing up the school!"

"Blow up mine, too," Madeleine cried out. "Especially Miss Raymond."

"Margaret Dumas, too," Lindsey said.

Suzi came skipping in, singing, "Margaret's in Lindsey's cla-aass . . . Margaret's in Lindsey's cla-aass . . ."

"*STOP!*" Lindsey burst into tears. "I *hate* her. She's my worst enemy."

Mary Anne put her arm around Lindsey. "I know how you feel."

"You do not," Lindsey said.

"This awful boy, Alan Gray, used to pull my hair all the time in second grade," Mary Anne continued. "He had another teacher, though, thank goodness. Well, the next September, in third grade, guess who was sitting right behind me in class?"

"Alan?" Lindsey said through sniffles.

Mary Anne nodded. "I cried for three days straight. Then my friend Kristy and I both told him off, and he never bothered me again."

"Really?"

Mary Anne nodded. "He bothered Kristy instead."

They both started laughing. (True story, by the way.)

"Blam! Stoneybrook Smellementary School bites the dust!" Buddy cried out.

Madeleine shuffled over to the couch and crawled under Mary Anne's other arm. "My tummy feels bad."

"She always says that," Suzi said, bouncing in again. "She's just mad she has to go to preschool."

"Boy, all of you are having back-to-school-itis, huh?" Mary Anne said. "Claudia and I will think of something fun to do."

Mary Anne looked over her shoulder. Through the open door, she could see the kitchen, but no Claudia. "Hmmm," she said, "who wants to play a game?"

"Candy Land!" Madeleine squealed.

"Me, too!" Suzi chimed in. She ran to the wall shelves, which are crammed with toys and games.

"Whoa, I just made five thousand points!" screamed Buddy the Game Boy addict, perfectly happy where he was.

Lindsey pulled a chessboard from the shelves. "Will you play with me?"

"Sure," Mary Anne said.

Suzi and Madeleine busily set up their

game. Lindsey was positioning her chess pieces. Buddy was blowing things up. The grumpy foursome was feeling a lot better.

Mary Anne was relieved. Mission accomplished.

After three chess moves, a loud thump sounded in the kitchen. Then Ryan's voice shrieked with delight.

"Have no fear, Claudia's here!" Claud shouted. "Art projects for everybody."

Claudia trudged into the family room, dragging a big, heavy bag. Taylor was struggling behind her with an easel. Ryan toddled along, pretending to help out.

"Look what we found," Claudia said. "Some plaster of paris, tempera paints, an easel. We can do painting, papier-mâché — "

She darted back into the kitchen, with Ryan skipping along behind.

"I hate papier-mâché," Buddy muttered.

"I like it," Suzi said. She stood up, knocking over a Candy Land piece.

"No fair!" Madeleine cried. "You just want to leave because you're losing!"

"Well, Claudia says we have to put it away now," Suzi announced.

"She didn't say that," Mary Anne said.

Claudia barged in, throwing a pile of old newspapers on the floor. "Buddy and Lindsey," Claudia called out, "you guys spread these out. We're going to need all the floor space, so pick up the games."

"We want to finish playing!" Lindsey said.

"We were in the middle of a good game," Mary Anne explained.

Claudia was already setting up the easel. "You can play checkers anytime, but art is something special. Besides, this'll stop you guys from arguing."

"But they weren't argu — " Mary Anne began.

Claudia zipped out of the room again and started clattering around in the kitchen.

"Let's just keep playing, Mary Anne," Lindsey said.

Before Mary Anne could answer, Claudia returned with a big bucket of water. "Uh, hello? Didn't I say to lay the papers down?"

Suzi started spreading the papers, kicking aside the Candy Land game.

Madeleine stood up and stormed away. Buddy wandered off, clutching his Game Boy. With a frustrated sigh, Lindsey carefully placed the chess game on the TV and followed Buddy.

"Guyyyys!" Claudia turned to Mary Anne, frowning. "Will you get them?"

"Well, maybe they want to do something else, Claudia — "

Claudia let out a funny kind of snort-laugh.

"Right. Puh-leeze. Like competitive games are going to stop them all from fighting?"

"It was working," Mary Anne insisted.

"Well, for a while, sure. But now they have something fun to do. Something cooperative. Creative." Claudia ripped open the plaster of paris bag. "Buddy! Lindsey! Madeleine! Come in here!"

Mary Anne took a deep breath. Then she let Claudia have it. Screamed at her. Threw the easel to the floor and dumped plaster of paris on her head.

Actually, that was what *I* would have done. But not Mary Anne. "Claudia," she said calmly, "art is great, but not everyone's so interested in it."

"Yeah?" Claudia said nonchalantly. "My parents, my sister, and who else?"

"Well, okay, if you want to know — me. And Buddy and Lindsey and Suzi and Madeleine. We were all in the middle of something we liked. I mean, if you had told us you were going to do this, we would have — "

CRAASSHHH!

"Marnie and Ryan dumped the dirty silverware out of the dishwasher!" Lindsey called out.

Mary Anne ran out of the room, calling over her shoulder, "Claudia, you should never leave the little ones all alone!"

Claudia followed her. The two-year-olds

were standing over a pile of dirty forks and spoons, laughing hysterically.

"They're okay," Claudia said.

"No thanks to you," Mary Anne commented under her breath.

"If you're so concerned, why don't you teach Marnie and Ryan to play Parcheesi?" Claudia said, marching out of the room.

"They're already making a silverware sculpture!" Mary Anne retorted.

(Boy, was Mary Anne furious. She *never* talks like that.)

She picked up the spilled silverware. She vowed not to go near Claudia the rest of the afternoon.

Fat chance. As soon as the art project began, the family room became complete chaos. Soon Mary Anne was breaking up a fight between Lindsey and Buddy. Then Buddy dumped papier-mâché on Madeleine's head, and you-know-who had to wash that off. Not to mention the purple and brown paint stains on the family room sofa, the windows, and her own brand-new cotton blouse.

By the time the job was finally over, the kids were all playing games again. Mary Anne could barely see straight. She wanted to explode at Claudia.

But she didn't have the chance. Claudia stormed away first, without saying good-bye.

CHAPTER 4

"A little lower," I called to Abby.

Claudia, Jessi, Mallory, Shannon, and I were standing under a maple tree in my front yard. Above us, Abby was clinging to a branch.

She turned a spool of string. The other end was tied to the stem of a red delicious apple. Slowly the apple dropped toward me.

"Stop there," I said.

The apple bobbed at about eye level.

"Now what?" Jessi asked.

"This is what all of McLelland Road will look like." I gestured up the road in front of my house. "A street full of apple trees. The kids will reach up and pick. Just like a trip to the orchard, only safer. Perfect, huh? A taste of the country in good old Stoneybrook — that's the motto of the Fall Into Fall Festival Block Party."

"Can I come down now?" Abby asked.

41

"It'll be easy and fun," I went on, yanking the apple off the string.

The branch wobbled. "Who-o-oa!" yelled Abby.

I looked up to see her hugging the branch for dear life . . . one hand holding the string I'd just pulled.

"Oops, sorry," I said. I bit into the apple and smiled at my friends. "Well, what do you think of my idea?"

Four open-mouthed stares answered me. My friends had become the Great American Gapers Association. GAGA.

It was Saturday, around ten o'clock in the morning. The sky was clear, and a cool northern breeze brought a hint of fall to the air. A perfect day for our first Fall Into Fall planning session.

Well, almost perfect. I'd sort of hoped that everyone would show up. But Stacey was off visiting her dad in New York, and Mary Anne said she wasn't feeling well. (Personally, I think she just didn't want to be near Claudia.)

I'd thought hard about the festival. We needed something creative and spectacular. In my opinion, the schedule shifting had been awful for club spirit. All three meetings that week had been tense. Claudia and Mary Anne weren't talking at all (Abby and I weren't exactly bosom buddies, either). Fall Into Fall was going to be a quadruple triumph — great for club morale, great for BSC public relations, great for the neighborhood kids, and a perfect way to publicize our schedule change.

For this, we would say good-bye to humdrum pumpkins and baked goods and leaf piles.

Apple-picking was just the first of my great ideas.

"It's . . ." Jessi said.

"It's . . ." Mallory echoed.

"Insane," Claudia finished.

"That's what they said about Picasso's theory of relativism," I said.

"You mean Einstein," Jessi said.

"Picasso's theory of Einstein," I corrected myself.

"I don't know about this, Kristy," Claudia said. "I mean, apples dangling over the street on strings? It'll look stupid."

"Not to mention all the time it'll take to set up," Shannon added.

Jessi nodded. "I have zero spare time, between homework and ballet practice, and — "

"We could just transplant a whole orchard," Abby suggested. "That would be less work."

"Don't worry, guys, you'll catch the spirit." I turned away and led them all toward the wooded area at the end of the block. "We need an open area for maple sugaring, so I figured this would do fine."

Claudia rubbed her ears. "I must need to have my hearing examined. I actually thought she said, 'maple sugaring.' Again."

"Kristy, be serious," Abby said.

"I am," I replied. "But the problem is, it takes, like, forty gallons of sap to make one gallon of maple syrup. So what we do is water down some real maple syrup, to make a kind of fake sap. Then we build a stone grill and make a fire, for boiling."

Claudia looked flabbergasted.

"Isn't it the wrong season for maple sugaring?" Shannon asked.

"Who cares?" I replied.

Mallory shook her head sadly. "I think she's lost it."

"What else, Kristy?" Abby laughed. "A laser light show?"

"A hay ride!" Jessi giggled. "With horses."

"Christmas lights will work just fine," I said. "But only the fall colors — orange, red, and white. We'll have to work on that. And Mrs. Stone has plenty of hay in her barn. I was thinking she could line the back of her pickup truck and drive the kids around. But horses — that's not a bad idea."

"I was only kidding!" Jessi said.

"Can't we just make it simple?" Mallory

pleaded. "Some leaf piles for jumping, some face-painting . . ."

"Bobbing for apples," Jessi suggested.

I sighed heavily. "You guys have no imagination. Follow me."

Tossing my apple from hand to hand, I led them all back into my house.

Watson was sipping coffee and reading the newspaper in the kitchen. He broke into a big smile. "Weekend meeting?"

"Nope," I answered. "Planning session for our gala Fall Into Fall Festival Block Party. Which wouldn't be complete without cider making."

Walking to the counter, I pulled out my mom's juice maker and dropped my apple into the hole at the top. I turned on the machine and it whirred to life. Most of the apple spat out, all mangled and chewed up, into a clear plastic pulp collector. A few drops of brown liquid plinked into the juice receptacle.

"Impressive," Abby said drily.

"Well, we'll need a lot of apples," I said. "So we'll start hanging them a few days in advance."

"Hanging them?" Watson repeated.

"From the trees outside," Claudia explained, shaking her head sadly. "For apple picking. It's part of the festival."

I described the plan to Watson. His reaction?

"Sounds . . . interesting. Did you set a date?"

"I was thinking, October fifth," I said.

"I guess you talked to the town about a permit?" Watson asked.

"Permit?" I repeated.

"You did say block party, right? I assume you want to close off the block? You do realize you have to apply for a permit to do that?"

Gulp.

"Of course I know," I lied. "I'll call the, uh, officials before our Monday meeting."

David Michael's voice filtered in through the open kitchen window. *"Hey, what's this string for?"*

My friends and I went outside. David Michael had run into the backyard with four friends: Hannie and Linny Papadakis, and Bill and Melody Korman.

I explained my idea to them. They seemed to like it, until I said I expected them to help set up.

"No way," said Hannie. "I'm not climbing trees. That's dangerous."

"Boiling syrup is boring," was Linny's contribution.

"You should hang candy instead," Melody suggested.

"Now, there's an idea," said Claudia. "We could turn the street into a candy mobile.

Change the theme. Call it Fall Into Abstract Edible Art or something."

Zing. Another idea hit me. "That's it, Claudia!"

"What's it?"

"Abstract art," I said. "We'll have a leaf sculpture! You know, like an ice sculpture, only better. Take some autumn leaves, pile them up, twine them together into big shapes or whatever. You'll be in charge of that part. Okay, now let's think of booths. We have to have some booths . . ."

Claudia was staring at me as if I'd just sprouted antennae.

Me? I didn't care. I had a festival to organize, and it was a month away. I was just warming up.

CHAPTER 5

"So, what elephants smelling maximum news and lottery?" asked my English teacher, Mr. Fiske.

Well, that was what it sounded like. I wasn't really paying attention. It was the Monday after our planning session and I was furiously scribbling ideas into my English notebook:

To do for FIFFBP
- hand pick or buy apples
  (3 bushels?)
  * find out how many are
    in a bushel *
- make sure leaf blower has gas
- buy Xmas lights
- real pumpkin masks?
- lighter fluid and coals

"Kristy?" Mr. Fiske said.

"Huh?"

The whole class was staring at me. Cokie Mason, the nemesis of my life, was snickering so hard her whole body was twitching. I must have looked like a total doofus.

Mr. Fiske let out a deep sigh. "One more time. What elements of storytelling does Shirley Jackson use in 'The Lottery'?"

"Elements?"

All I could think of were hydrogen and oxygen. I had to remind myself which class I was in.

"Theme? Point of view? Use of irony?" Mr. Fiske pressed on. "Did you find this to be a morality tale, Kristy, or was it a simple horror story?"

I'd read "The Lottery." It was a weird story with a surprise ending (I won't spoil it for you), which I liked a lot.

"Well," I ventured. "Uh, it was pretty cool, actually . . ."

Cokie shot her hand into the air.

"Cokie?" Mr. Fiske asked.

"I wasn't fin — " I protested.

"*Shirl*ey Jackson does *not* take the *point* of view of *any* character," Cokie read in a singsong voice from a sheet of looseleaf paper, "thus *height*ening the *narr*ative distance and *giv*ing the story a *ten*sion which *builds* until the *fin*al shock, de*liv*ering a *pow*erful *mor*al message about *mass* psychology in *Amer*ican society."

Mr. Fiske smiled. "Excellent analysis. Does

anyone have anything to add to that?"

As he walked across the room, Cokie crossed her eyes at me.

I was steaming. I wouldn't have said exactly that (I didn't know what it meant), but at least I would have used my own words. I just knew she had copied that answer out of some book. Cokie's not that smart. Besides, she's a cheater, a liar, and the world's laziest student.

Otherwise, she's a lovely person.

Mr. Fiske looked at the clock. "Tonight we descend further into gothic territory. Please read Poe's 'The Fall of the House of Usher' by tomorrow. For those of you who may be thinking of other pursuits . . ." He gave me a look, and suddenly I had the urge to hurl my textbook at Cokie. "I must remind you that you will have a reading assignment every night *and* over each weekend. Fall behind, and you will sink fast. Stay with me, and you'll be richly rewarded, as we visit the vastly different worlds of Dickens, Stevenson, Faulkner, Blume, Cormier . . ."

With each name, my heart sank. Not that I hate reading. I like it. But this was serious stuff. How was I going to do all of it and babysit?

After class I slumped into the hallway, avoiding eye contact with Cokie. Fortunately, the next period was lunch. Mary Anne, as usual, was waiting for me by her locker.

"Uh-oh," she asked. "What's wrong?"

I shrugged. "Nothing a terrible hot lunch can't cure. I just can't believe how much work I have to do this year."

"Me, too," Mary Anne said as we walked toward the cafeteria. "My science teacher is making us collect specimens and set up a home lab . . ."

Mary Anne's sentence trailed off. She was staring at a huge poster on the bulletin board outside the cafeteria. In splashy red letters, STONEYBROOK FALL FROLIC was printed over a background of bright, colorful leaves.

" 'A day of autumn crafts and events,' " I read aloud. " 'Brenner Field. Saturday, October fifth.' *Whaaaat?* That was the day for Fall Into Fall! How could they do this to me?"

"Oh, Kristy, don't be upset," Mary Anne said. "Maybe it's just as well. I mean, we're all kind of tired from the Mexican festival. No one will be disappointed if we don't do it — "

"Who said anything about not doing it?" I asked. "We'll postpone it until the twelfth. The trees will be more colorful, anyway."

"Uh-huh," Mary Anne said dully.

We stepped onto the lunch line. I grabbed

a tray and slapped it onto the metal track. "You make it sound as if no one wants to do Fall Into Fall," I remarked.

"I didn't say that. It's just that everyone is busy, Kristy. You said yourself that school is going to be a lot of work this year."

As Mary Anne was loading up her tray, I spotted Claudia entering the line. "Hi, Claud!" I called out.

Mary Anne's face froze. She quickly picked up her tray and scooted toward the tables.

I took a couple of frozen yogurts and followed her.

The usual BSC table was empty. Mary Anne sat at the end of it. I sat to her left.

"Don't let her near me," Mary Anne whispered.

"Can't you guys just kiss and make up?" I asked.

"Ask Claudia. She's the one who decided not to talk to me."

"Well, you weren't exactly Miss Congeniality yourself."

"*Gene*. Congeniality."

"Whatever."

Claudia sat down across the table from me, two seats to my left. She gave me a tight-lipped smile and said hello.

"Hmm, I have this crick in my neck when I turn your way, Claud. Maybe you can slide over a few seats closer to my friend, Mary Anne.''

I thought a little humor wouldn't hurt. Boy, was I wrong. Claudia frowned and dug into her sandwich. Mary Anne began twirling her pasta onto a fork.

''Hey, guys, anyone know what's between the bread today?'' Abby's voice called out.

She and Stacey sat down directly opposite me, creating a kind of buffer zone between the enemy camps.

Abby lifted a slice of bread from her sandwich and examined the brown glop inside. ''So that's what they did with last year's footballs.''

Stacey nodded. ''Recycling.''

Claudia and Mary Anne silently chewed their meals. They looked like the faces on the rocks at Easter Island.

''Did you see that poster?'' Abby asked. ''Guess we're off, huh?''

''Nah,'' I replied. ''We'll do it the week after.''

Mary Anne shook her head. ''We can't. Mallory and her family are visiting cousins in Pennsylvania.''

''Janine's getting a certificate from the chamber of commerce that day,'' Claudia muttered. ''Genius of the decade or something.''

I shrugged. ''Okay, then, the week after.''

Abby took a date book from her backpack

and leafed through it. "We're visiting my uncle on Long Island that weekend."

"The *next* week," I pressed on.

"That's the last weekend in October," Stacey said. "My dad's taking me apple picking in the country."

Abby laughed. "How about a Thanksgiving festival instead?"

"Fall Into Winter," Stacey suggested.

"We could hang snowballs from the trees," Claudia said.

Everyone was cracking up now. No one seemed concerned about our crisis.

"Don't you guys *want* to do this?" I asked.

No one answered right away. They were all looking at each other. Trying not to smile.

I could take the hint.

"Great, guys," I said. "Just great. I go through all the trouble to think up the most fantastic event in BSC history, and no one wants to do it. Forget it, then. It won't work if I'm the only one interested."

I shoved a hunk of hamburger in my mouth.

"It's not that, Kristy," Mary Anne said.

"Oh, yes, it is," Abby piped up.

I glared at her. "What's with you guys? Don't you want to get the year off to a good start?"

"Sure," Abby said. "But Kristy, you have to face facts. If we can't do it, we can't do it.

As my dad used to say, 'You have to meet your overhead and move on.' "

"What's overhead?" Claudia asked.

Abby looked up. "A roof."

"Oh!" Claudia blurted out. "Mary Anne, I forgot to tell you. I have a dentist appointment on Wednesday afternoon. Dr. Rice could only make an appointment during meeting time."

"I have a problem, too," Stacey said. "With Monday. My doctor wants me to come in for a checkup."

Mary Anne scribbled notes on the back of a napkin.

Abby cleared her throat. "While we're on the subject, what if marching band practice goes past five-thirty? Can I, like, have a lateness clause?"

"Marching band?" I asked. "Is this some kind of joke?"

Abby shrugged. "I'm thinking of it. Anna says I should start on an instrument."

What was going on here? Had the Baby-sitters Club suddenly dropped to bottom priority? I wanted to jump up and scream at them.

I counted to twenty in my head, then said, "I knew when we changed our schedule, something like this would happen."

Stacey rolled her eyes. "Kristy, one thing has nothing to do with the other."

"Remember when Monday, Wednesday, and Friday used to be untouchable?" I asked. "We set up our appointments and stuff around meeting times. Gladly. Because we knew we had to. That was why I didn't want to change Fridays. Once you do something like that, you're saying the club isn't that important. Now look what's happening — a chain reaction."

"Uh, I think you may be taking this a little too seriously," Claudia said.

"Our clients depend on us," I shot back. "That's why they keeping calling back. Our motto was 'One call, seven sitters' — remember? Not 'one call, four or five sitters who bothered to show up and a couple of others out shopping.' "

"Kristy, our clients don't care who's actually at the meeting," Stacey said. "They can't see us."

"I never understood why we have to be so strict about attendance," Abby added. "Mary Anne can book an absent member for a job."

"When you think about it, we could have the club with no members present at all," Claudia remarked. "Just let the answering machine pick up. I mean, we always take their information and call back anyway."

"Oh, great, Claudia," I said. "So why bother having meetings at all?"

"Hey, relax, I wasn't serious," Claudia replied. "I just meant that we can be flexible. We're busy people, Kristy. We have to bend a little."

I pushed my chair back and stood up. "Look. I invented the Baby-sitters Club. The whole idea was to work together. Human-to-human contact, over the phone and in meetings. If you don't have that, you don't have a club. Period."

"Kristy — " Mary Anne pleaded.

But I'd heard enough. I picked up my tray and walked away.

I had completely lost my appetite.

CHAPTER 6

"Kristy, look!" called Jackie Rodowsky.

My back was to him. I was busy gassing up Archie Rodowsky's toy car with a garden hose (shut off, of course).

"Vroom! Vroom! High octame, please!" ordered Archie.

Jackie is seven and Archie's four. I was sitting for them Tuesday afternoon because their parents and their nine-year-old brother, Shea, were at a teacher conference.

Actually, Shannon was supposed to have taken the job, but she had to cancel. She'd called during our meeting to tell me that she now had astronomy club on Tuesdays.

Surprised we'd had a meeting the afternoon of our cafeteria fight? I was.

I, Nerves-of-Steel Thomas, had a lump in my throat when I went to Claudia's house. I half expected to find a Keep Out sign on her

58

door and a voodoo ritual with a Kristy doll going on inside.

It wasn't that bad.

Everyone apologized to me, and I forgave them. We paid dues, took a few calls, and went home. A nice, normal meeting.

Sort of.

Claudia and Mary Anne still weren't speaking to each other. Every time I looked at Abby, I could feel something clench up in my stomach. Stacey spent most of her time huddled over a math book with Claudia, giving homework advice. Jessi did a ballet warmup that took up half the room and lasted the whole meeting. Mallory had her nose in a book.

I wouldn't put it on my list of best meetings, but at least we weren't screaming at each other. I was kind of relieved.

"Krist*yyyyyy*!" Jackie shouted again.

"Just a minute!" I withdrew the garden hose from the gas tank of Archie's plastic car. "All full, sir. That'll be ten dollars!"

"No, ten cents!" Archie said, and he drove away without paying. (Sometimes the young ones are the toughest customers.)

I turned to see Jackie sitting in the fork of the Rodowskys' old oak tree, about four feet off the ground. His gap-toothed grin made him look like a jack-o'-lantern. "I climbed up here all by myself!"

"Great, Jackie," I said. "Just don't go up any higher."

"I'm going to hang a googolplex apples!"

"Uh, Jackie, I hate to tell you this, but the festival is off."

The jack-o'-lantern disappeared. "Why?"

"There's going to be another fair the same day, at Brenner Field," I explained.

"Then I'll hang apples there!"

"Jackie, I don't want you climbing any higher. It's too dangerous."

"But I want to!"

"Get down!"

"No!"

Out of the corner of my eye, I could see Archie vrooming along the driveway, around the corner of the house. I thought fast. "Jackie, is it that you don't know how to climb down? I could help you . . . "

That did it. Down he came.

I should explain something. Jackie Rodowsky's private BSC nickname is the Walking Disaster. Abby says he has the Sadim touch. Sadim is Midas backward. Everything he touches turns into an accident.

He has had a raisin stuck up his nose. He's poked himself in the eye with a drinking straw. He's had his arm stuck in his pants drawer. I can't count how many times he's been in a cast.

Seeing him in a tree hadn't done much for my nerves of steel. Now that he was climbing down, I raced away. "Archie, where are you going?" I yelled out.

He was rolling down the driveway, toward the street. "Shopping," he announced.

"Oh. Well, the store's that way," I said, pointing toward the backyard.

Archie stopped. Sighing heavily, he said, "Not *that* store. The supermarker."

"Oh, of course." I called into the backyard: "Jackie, are you on solid ground yet?"

"Ye-es!" sang Jackie.

"Park right here, sir," I said to Archie. "Step in for our specials on chicken and marshmallows."

Archie solemnly climbed out of his car and strode up the front lawn with me. "Do you sell trucks?"

"Uh, why, sure we do. Right back here near the dairy products."

Archie took an imaginary shopping cart and started loading it up. As I waited by the imaginary checkout counter, I heard Jackie's voice above me: "Hey, Kristy! I'm climbing on the roof!"

My heart nearly jumped into the cash register. I looked up, shielding my eyes from the sun. "Jackie, don't you dare — "

Jackie grinned at me from behind the screen of a second-story window. "Fooled you!"

"Not funny," I said.

Archie jumped up and down, clapping his hands. "Do it!"

"You stay out of this," I said. "You're shopping."

Archie sighed. "Do I have enough to buy a tree?" he asked, holding out imaginary money.

"Sure."

As Archie and I bagged his purchases, I kept glancing up at the bedroom window.

While we were loading the car, I heard the *whack* of the back door slamming. Good, I thought. Jackie was back on solid ground.

I trotted alongside Archie as he rode up the driveway and into the backyard.

Jackie wasn't anywhere to be seen. My eyes darted toward the toolshed, but the door was bolted shut.

Archie parked his car near the garden hose and climbed out. An acorn bounced off the roof of his car.

"Hey!" He looked around, startled.

"Just a squirrel," I reassured him.

And then another acorn bopped me on the head.

I heard giggling overhead. I looked up.

Through the leafy branches of the maple tree, I could see Jackie. He was hanging onto a branch at least the height of a basketball rim.

"*Jackie, what are you doing up there?*" I yelled.

"Look!" he cried out, waving his arms crazily. "I can hang on with just my legs!"

His right arm clipped a small overhead branch. His body lurched off balance. His smile vanished.

"*Jackie, noooo!*"

He fell forward, lunging with his arms. His palms slapped against the branch next to him.

For a moment he balanced himself, stretched between the two branches. His face was frozen with fright. Then his fingers began to slip. I ran toward him, arms outstretched.

But I was too late. With a high-pitched scream, Jackie tumbled out of the tree.

He hit the ground with a thud.

I dropped onto my knees by Jackie's side. "Are you all right?"

All I could hear was Archie, wailing at the top of his lungs.

Jackie was silent. His eyes were open, but he didn't seem to notice me. I leaned over him. "Jackie?"

He sat up suddenly, looking disoriented. Then his face crumpled and he burst into hysterical tears.

Relief washed over me. Jackie was conscious. He was able to move. His back seemed okay.

I wrapped him in a big hug. Over my shoulder, poor Archie was shrieking as if his brother had died. "He's okay," I said, signaling him over.

Archie threw his arms around Jackie from behind.

"Can you bend your arms and legs?" I asked.

Jackie wiggled his arms. They seemed fine. But when he raised his left leg, he grimaced. "*OW!* My ankle!"

"Put your left arm around my shoulder," I said.

I carefully helped him up. "Ow ow ow ow!" he screamed.

Leaning on me, Jackie was able to hop to a picnic bench.

Half of me wanted to throttle him. The other half wanted to scream at myself.

I was Jackie's sitter. I was responsible for him. Sure I warned him. Sure he was being obnoxious. But the bottom line was, he was injured. And I was not supposed to let that happen.

"Is his leg breaked?" Archie asked.

"I don't know," I replied. "Jackie, try to point your toes and then pull your foot back."

His face was twisted with pain, but he was

able to do it. "Do I have to go to the doctor?" he whimpered.

"Probably." I checked my watch. "But we can wait until your mom and dad come home. Meanwhile let's put some ice on it."

I helped him inside and laid him down on the family room sofa. Then I found a blue-liquid cold pack in the Rodowskys' freezer and wrapped it around his ankle with a dish towel.

I let Jackie and Archie watch a video while I monitored the ankle. It swelled a bit, but it didn't look too horrible.

When I heard the Rodowskys' car pull into the driveway, my stomach jumped.

In third grade, I beat up a boy who was teasing me in the school playground. I actually gave him a black eye. That evening his parents brought him to my house, just to yell at me. I will never forget the sinking feeling I had when I saw them walking up the front path.

That was exactly how I was feeling when the Rodowskys came into the family room.

As I explained everything, Mr. Rodowsky listened stonily. Shea had that *There goes Jackie again* look. Mrs. Rodowsky knelt down and felt Jackie's forehead (why do parents always do that?).

"That ankle will have to be looked at," Mr. Rodowsky said.

Jackie started to cry.

"I'm so sorry, Mrs. Rodowsky," I said. "It's my fault. I should have kept Jackie and Archie together, so I could see them both. I never should have let Jackie out of my sight."

Mrs. Rodowsky gave me a tight smile. "It's not your fault, Kristy. Kids will be kids."

I knew she meant *Jackie will be Jackie*. I knew she understood Jackie's accident-prone personality. But he was her son. And I was the baby-sitter.

All this BSC pressure was getting to me. I was forgetting how to be a good sitter.

Or maybe I had never been one to begin with. Maybe that's why the club was falling apart.

Maybe I needed to back off baby-sitting for awhile.

As I walked home, I felt about two inches tall.

CHAPTER 7

"So, if 3x equals 24 and 7x equals y," Stacey said, looking up from Claudia's textbook, "then you have to solve equations for two different variables."

"Why?" Claudia asked.

"Right," Stacey said. "And x."

"No, I mean, *why* do I have to solve equations? Can't I just, like, try out numbers and see if they work?"

I drummed my fingers against Claudia's dresser. It was 5:35 on Wednesday, and the meeting had turned into a study hall.

Logan and Shannon were both there, which was a nice change of pace, although he was reading a paperback, and she was memorizing French vocabulary words. Jessi and Mallory were going over their social studies homework. As for Mary Anne and Abby? Well, for all I knew, they were staying after school for remedial help of their own. They sure weren't at the meeting.

Had either of them called? No. Had an official conflict been recorded for either of them in the BSC record book? No. They were just late. Plain and simple.

I hate lateness. Especially unexcused lateness. I was stewing, big-time.

Honestly, I didn't need any extra aggravation. The day had been bad enough. I'd called the Rodowskys and found out that Jackie's ankle had been pretty badly sprained (though not broken, thank goodness), and he would have to use a cane for awhile.

Mrs. Rodowsky had been polite to me over the phone, but I could tell she wasn't thrilled. I apologized about a million times.

I felt like a fool. A rotten sitter. Kristy the Careless. Everyone in town was going to see Jackie with his cane. Of course they would ask what happened.

And they'd find out the truth. He'd been left unsupervised by his sitter in his own backyard.

If there were such things as sitting licenses, mine would be revoked.

"Well," I said, "I can't wait forever for Mary Anne and Abby. Any new business?"

"Tell her, Mallory," I heard Jessi whisper.

Mallory's face was beet red.

"Tell me what?" I asked.

Mallory adjusted her glasses. "Well, um, it's just that . . . I don't have to do it, but I was asked to join this group at the Stoneybrook Public Library. It's a creative writing group, and we have to write a complete short story, and it lasts for six weeks."

"Great," I said. "When does it meet?"

"Uh, that's the thing. I mean, like I said, I don't have to do it. But it's kind of what I want to do more than anything else in my life and the teacher is fantastic and — "

"When, Mal?" I pressed.

She scratched her chin, blocking her mouth. "Wezoo forver zhuck."

"What?" I asked.

"Wednesday from four-thirty to six," Jessi clarified.

"But that's a meeting time," I said.

Mallory just nodded.

"I told her she should bring it up now, while the year is just beginning," Jessi said. "See, if we switch our Wednesday meeting to Tuesday, we can put that information in the fliers we already put up, and our customers will know all our changes at once."

"No," I said flatly.

"I think it sounds like a great opportunity," Shannon spoke up.

"Maybe we can just agree to excuse Mallory

on Wednesdays until the program is over," Stacey suggested.

"Let's put it to a vote," Claudia said.

"Uh, excuse me, we can't," I said. "Doesn't anyone notice that we are missing two members at the moment?"

Claudia looked around. "Okay, we'll wait."

"Isn't anyone disturbed about this?" I pressed on.

"They'll show up," Jessi said with a shrug. *Rrrrring!*

I snatched up the receiver. "Baby-sitters Club!"

"Yes, hello, Kristy, this is Mrs. Papadakis. Am I calling at a bad time?"

"No!" I shouted. "I mean, no. What can I do for you?"

"I need a sitter for Monday evening. About six-thirty to nine."

"I'll check and call you back, okay?"

We said good-bye and hung up. Normally, at times like this, Mary Anne picks up the record book and checks the calendar. If she's absent, Abby the alternate officer performs that duty.

But both our secretary and our alternate were inexplicably absent, and the book was just lying there. And now everyone was busy chatting with Mallory about her new "opportunity," as if no call had come in at all.

"Please don't all reach for this at once," I said, picking up the record book.

The door flew open. "Hi! Sorry we're late."

Mary Anne bustled across the room with a sheepish smile and sat on the floor next to Logan. Behind her, Abby was leaning down to give Jessi and Mallory a backward low-five.

The moment Claudia saw Mary Anne, her face turned stony. She buried it in her math book without saying hello.

"Sorry, by fault," Abby said, her voice all stuffed up. "I was school shoppig. Bary Add was school shoppig. We bet. We talked. I had to buy a dress so Bary Add helped. Thed I had ad allergic reactiod to — "

"I guess all the pay phones at the mall were out of order?" I said. "Or did you spend your last quarter on the dress?"

Abby and Mary Anne just stared at me, squirming.

Okay, so I sounded cold. I couldn't help it.

I am a reasonable person. Really. Even about latenesses. That is, if a BSC member has a good reason, like an accident or a death or a horrible family crisis.

But a *shopping trip*?

I was seeing red.

"Mrs. Papadakis already called," I continued, running my finger across the calendar, "and she needs someone on Monday evening.

71

And we have to vote on whether to change *another* meeting day because of a writing group Mallory wants to join."

Mary Anne sat at the edge of Claudia's bed, on the verge of tears. Mallory looked mortified. Abby plopped down next to her and said, "Cool. Are they goigg to get you a publishigg deal?"

"*Abby's available*," I said loudly.

"Uh-uh, dot the Papadakises," Abby protested. "They have a cat *add* a dog. I'll be sdeezigg all week."

" 'Jessi — the Hobarts,' " I read. " 'Mallory — orthodontist. Mary Anne — Prezziosos. Logan — practice. Shannon — honor society.' How about you, Claudia?"

Claudia grimaced. "I have a math quiz the next day. I need time to study."

"Stacey?" I asked.

"Uh, well, my mom was asked to go to this fashion show for retail buyers, and she asked if I wanted to go. I was going to tell you, but — "

"Never mind," I snapped. "I guess I'll have to do it."

"Whoa, Kristy, chill," Abby said. "Takigg a sittigg job is ad okay thigg. We *are* the Baby-sitters Club."

"Thank you soooo much for reminding me,

Abby," I replied. "Maybe you should have thought of that at the mall."

"Kristy, what's gotted idto you?" Abby asked.

"We said we were sorry," Mary Anne reminded me.

"Yeah, I know you did. I guess I'm just upset. I don't know why. Maybe it's because the club is falling apart before my eyes. Maybe it's that I put Jackie Rodowsky in the hospital yesterday. Maybe — "

"Whoa, whoa, backtrack a bidit," Abby said. "What happedd at the Rodowskys'?"

I finally explained the whole ugly job. Abby listened carefully and said, "Doe wodder you're acting like a jerk today. I'd be upset, too."

"Typical Jackie," Logan added.

Rrrring!

Claudia picked up the phone. "Hello, Baby-sitters Club! Oh, hi, Mrs. Korman . . . When? This Friday? I'll call you back."

Mary Anne took the record book from me and looked up the date. "Let's see . . . Jessi — ballet lesson; Abby, Kristy, Stacey, Claudia, and I — Anna's recital; Mallory — the movies with her family; Shannon — drama club meeting." She frowned. "Logan — practice."

I was fuming. Speechless.

"Uh-oh," Stacey said.

"Baybe Dawd will agree to fly out for this," Abby suggested.

"You could take the kids to the recital," Mallory suggested.

"Good idea," Abby said. "I'll ask theb to brigg kazoos. They cad play along with Adda on the Beethovedd."

Claudia did an imitation of a kazoo playing some classical music. Jessi stood up and started dancing.

I unclenched my jaw. "I'll take the Korman job, too."

"But what about the recital?" Abby asked.

"I have my priorities," I shot back. "Unlike some people I know."

Abby glared at me. "Oh, right, Kristy. Like I shouldd't go to by ode sister's codcert."

"I wasn't talking about you," I said.

"No, she was just dumping on the rest of us," Stacey said.

"Uh, excuse me, Kristy," Claudia said, "we know you're mad at yourself for messing up at the Rodowskys', but don't take it out on us."

"*This has nothing to do with the Rodowskys!*" I shouted. "This has to do with all of you. What are we here for, guys? To sit around, do homework, and talk about all our great activities?"

"Souds like fud to be," Abby remarked.

"Lots of *fud*, Abby," I said. "So who needs meeting times and rules and stuff? Why not just hang out any old time? And skip the sitting part. That just gets in the way of the *fud*. I mean, no one has time to sit anymore. I might as well split off by myself. I'll be Kristy's Sitting Service. That's what we're turning into, anyway."

All eyes were on me. Wide and stunned.

"Whoa, easy, Kristy," Logan said.

"Kristy, I don't believe you," Mary Anne whispered. "That was mean."

"Look," I said evenly, "I don't mean to be a jerk. I know this is supposed to be a club. And a club is supposed to be fun. But we're a service, too. A service that relies on happy, steady clients. To keep them, we have to hold up our end of the bargain. And that means sticking to meeting times, being here when clients call, and showing good attitude, all the time. If I'm the only one with an open enough schedule — me, Kristy the incompetent, specializing in injured kids — then what's the point? We might as well disband the club. The end. 'Bye-'bye."

"Kristy, aren't you going overboard?" Shannon said.

"Maybe you need to lie down," Claudia suggested.

You know what? I didn't need to lie down. And I wasn't going overboard.

My anger was lifting. In my mind, the choices were becoming crystal clear. "I mean this, guys. It's the beginning of the school year. If things are this bad now, they're only going to become worse. Before too long, we won't be speaking to each other. I'd rather we broke up the club and saved our friendships."

No one said a word for what seemed like hours.

Finally Stacey spoke up. "We could still baby-sit, you know."

"It just wouldn't take up so much time," Claudia added.

Jessi was shaking her head, stunned. "You're taking her seriously!"

"What happened to 'One call, seven sitters'?" Mallory asked. "How can we take that away from our clients?"

"But they know us all now," Abby said. "They can reach any one of us at home."

"And they wouldn't have to call just during meeting times," Shannon went on. "Some people would prefer that, I'm sure."

"Look, I take back what I said about the writing group, okay?" Mallory blurted out. "I didn't meant to start anything."

"This isn't because of you, Mallory," I said. "If it didn't happen today, it would have happened another day. No group lasts forever, right? Maybe it's just time."

"Okay, okay, let's just chill a minute," Jessi said, standing up. "Kristy's saying this because she's upset. That's cool. But come on, now — Mary Anne, Claudia, Stacey, you guys were all there with Kristy at the beginning. You can't let it all go. Can you?"

Mary Anne and Stacey gave each other a silent, guilty Look.

Claudia let out a little laugh. "I know this sounds weird, but I feel . . . relieved."

"Should we vote od it?" Abby asked.

My heart felt as if it were being hit with a hammer. The BSC — *my* BSC, the center of my life, was about to come to an end. A voice inside was screaming to stop this nonsense, say it was all a joke.

But I knew this was the right thing to do.

I took two long, deep breaths. "All in favor of disbanding the Baby-sitters Club raise your hands."

Not one hand went up.

Then, shakily, Claudia raised hers.

Stacey's followed. Then Abby's and Shannon's.

I swallowed hard. I shot mine in the air.

Logan followed. Mary Anne burst into tears as she put hers up.

Jessi and Mallory were crying, too. Both of

their arms were folded tightly against their chests.

"I — " The words caught in my throat. "I, Kristy Thomas, hereby declare that the Baby-sitters Club no longer exists."

As soon as the words left my mouth, I wanted to pass out.

But I didn't. I just looked from one pair of teary eyes to the next. Nobody seemed to know what to say.

Except Claudia. She blew her nose, then leaned over to her answering machine and pressed the record button.

"Hello, this is Claudia," she said softly. "The Baby-sitters Club is no longer in existence, but individual members are available at their home numbers. Please leave a message for me at the sound of the beep . . ."

CHAPTER 8

I am a morning person.

Some people spill out of bed, grumpy and cross. Not me. I'm happy and alert. My mind races along, picturing all the things I have to do during the day.

I've always been that way, except for two times in my life. The first was when my dad left our family. I'd pop out of bed, raring to go, and then *WHAM!* The awful memory would come flooding in.

The second time? Right then. The ABSC era. After Baby-sitters Club.

The morning after the big BSC split, I woke up feeling great. But as soon as my feet hit the floor, my brain shifted into gear.

What have I done?

The question was like a cold slap in the face. My stomach knotted right up.

No Baby-sitters Club. No meetings to run.

No schedule to keep track of. No group to plan events for.

I felt as if a huge chunk had been carved out of me.

I threw on some clothes and slumped downstairs. Mom was bustling around the kitchen and Watson was at the stove, making breakfast. David Michael was wolfing down a bowl of cereal, and Nannie was helping Emily Michelle with her breakfast.

" 'Morning!" Watson chirped as I peered over his shoulder. "Want first taste of the bacon?"

"That's not fair!" shouted Sam from upstairs.

"No, thanks," I said. I love bacon, but somehow the thought of it that morning made me nauseous.

"No?" Watson looked shocked. "She must be sick! Call the medics!"

"I'll have some," David Michael piped up.

As Watson served him, I rustled up a breakfast of Rice Krispies.

Mom gave me a sympathetic smile. "Still thinking about the Baby-sitters Club, sweetheart?"

Yes, I had told her about it. What a roller coaster the previous evening had been. I kept second-guessing my decision. Half the time I'd wanted to call every BSC member and say,

"Just kidding!" The other half I'd felt this sense of relief. Yes, relief. It was faint, but it was definitely there.

"I guess," I said.

"Listen, if you're upset about it, why not just call this a trial period?" Mom suggested. "Give yourselves a few months or so."

I thought about that. I imagined reestablishing the club again in the wintertime. Convincing everyone to join again (or finding new members). Notifying our clients. Arranging our meeting days around everyone's conflicts.

No way.

I had to face facts. The club had changed from a big joy to a big pain. It was time to move on.

Charlie and Sam came clumping downstairs. "If you ate all the bacon, I'll kill you!" Sam roared.

I licked my chops. "It sure was good."

Charlie darted around Watson and peeked at the stove. "Yyyyes!"

Sam sneered at me. "You'd better be nice to us, Kristy. Especially now that you're going to be in our faces a lot."

Charlie laughed. "I give her a week before she's running back to the BSC."

"Five days," Sam said.

"Two minutes," David Michael chimed in.

"Guyyys," Watson warned.

"Trist-teeeee! Trist-teeeee!" Emily Michelle squealed. "Tiss!"

Good old Emily Michelle. Her lips were totally crudded up with bananas and oatmeal, and she was puckering for a kiss. (This is her latest habit. She thinks it's hilarious.)

"Ewwwwww!" I cried out.

Emily shrieked with laughter.

Nannie chuckled and gave me a wink. My brothers were attacking the bacon like cavemen who hadn't seen a meal in weeks. Mom had her arm around Watson, who was now making more oatmeal.

Me? My bad mood was flying out the kitchen window.

Despite my brothers.

Sam was right, in his own horrible way. Without the BSC, I would be spending more time with my family. My life was going to be simpler now. School and home. With babysitting as a sideline. A hobby, not an obsession.

I could get to like this.

"Why are you giving us that goony smile?" Charlie grumbled.

"She wants to make us barf with her ugly face, so she can eat the rest of the bacon," David Michael replied.

When I knew Mom and Watson and Nannie

weren't looking, I flung soggy Rice Krispies at them both.

My good nature does have its limits.

As I approached school that day, my knees were shaking.

I know what you're thinking. Kristy the Lion-Hearted, scared? Impossible.

Well, I was, so get over it.

No, I hadn't changed my mind. I was confident our breakup was the right thing to do (as painful as it was). But I also knew my friends. They would be basket cases. How could I deal with their tearful faces, their pleas to reconsider?

I do have a heart. And I was worried it would be swayed. I did not want to backslide.

As I approached Mary Anne at her locker, before homeroom, I prepared myself for the waterfall.

"Hi, Mary Anne," I said.

She turned around. Her eyes locked with mine.

Don't give in, I told myself. It's all for the best.

"I am so upset," she began.

"Mary Anne, we discussed this, and — "

"They're serving shell pasta with pesto sauce for lunch," she continued.

"Oh . . . um, too bad."

"I think they dilute that stuff with spinach or something," she said. "It's awful."

We walked toward homeroom. We did not mention the BSC once. (Duh. Did I feel like a fool.)

I figured maybe Mary Anne had cried herself out. She was so torn apart inside, she just couldn't show the pain anymore.

I began to worry about her.

You know what? Stacey, Claudia, and Abby weren't showing much pain either. At least none of them came up to me in the hallways on their hands and knees with bloodshot eyes and clasped hands.

No begging. No backsliding. Nothing. For awhile I thought the whole thing might have been a dream.

Finally, at lunch, we did discuss the breakup. Calmly. Maturely. With disappointment but relief.

I didn't see Jessi and Mallory until after school. They were still upset. I think they were worried our friendships would fall apart.

Before I caught my bus to go home, we all said we'd try to get together over the weekend. Then we said a nice, calm good-bye.

How did I feel, on a day that used to be a BSC meeting day?

Like a mixed-vegetable ice cream sundae —

full of good and bad things that didn't mix at all.

Boy, was it weird to know I wouldn't be heading to Claudia's. My mind was still in auto-BSC-mode — anxious to finish my homework before meeting time, worrying whether Charlie's car was in the shop for repairs.

Relax, I told myself.

Part of me had hoped my BSC friends had planned this whole thing as a huge April Fool's joke, seven months early. We'd all have a big laugh and go back to the way we were, loyal and full of group spirit.

But here's the other side: even though my mind was a mess, my body felt the strangest sense of calmness. As if I'd just taken a swim on a Hawaiian beach.

I felt free. Free and peaceful.

A few seats in front of me, Abby was laughing about something with Anna. They both looked so happy. Why shouldn't they? They'd be seeing more of each other now. (Also, Abby wouldn't have to worry about being president ever again — thank goodness.)

I smiled. I pursed my lips to whistle a tune, but then I stopped myself.

I mean, let's not get carried away. The BSC had ended. This was not exactly a time to be joyous.

When I was dropped off, I breezed into my

house and kissed my little brother hello. Why? I don't know. I just felt like it.

He screamed and ran into the bathroom to wash his face.

I had a leisurely snack. I read the sports pages. I played with Emily. I played with Shannon, our puppy. I greeted my big brothers as they gallumphed home from school.

I even went outside to help out in Watson's garden. For me, this is a big deal. I find gardening about as exciting as reading the phone book. But I figured, hey, it was a gorgeous, clear day. I was *free*.

I didn't mind gardening at all. In fact, it was kind of fun. For awhile.

As I was yanking a beet out of the ground, I started feeling funny. A little nauseous and shaky.

I glanced at my watch.

It was five-thirty.

I gulped. My instincts were telling me to be at Claud's. The words *I call this meeting to order* were trying desperately to climb out of my mouth.

It was now official. The BSC was an ex-club.

I felt as if a beet had jumped into my throat.

Rrrrrring! sounded the kitchen phone.

An irate BSC customer! Had to be. He or she had called Claudia's number, found out the news, and was now ready to scream at me. I had to pick up the call before an innocent family member was caught in the crossfire.

I raced inside and grabbed the receiver.

"Hello, Baby — I mean, hello!"

"Hi, Kristy." The voice was faint and sad, but I recognized it.

"Mallory?" I said.

"Uh-huh. Um, I was thinking maybe we could all get together. Not in Claudia's room, but somewhere else. Just so we can have the feeling of being friends, without being a club." She fell silent for awhile. "It's kind of hard to just stop cold, you know."

I felt bad. Somehow the breakup was hitting her and Jessi the worst. If *I* was feeling a pang, those two must have been pretty devastated.

"Sure, Mal," I said. "Let me call everyone and get back to you."

We hung up, and I immediately tried Mary Anne. Sharon, her stepmother, answered and said she was out with Logan.

The next person I tried was Stacey. No answer.

I kept calling. Abby was about to go shopping with her mom. Jessi was out. Claudia was being tutored by Janine *and* her dad.

I had to call Mallory back and break the bad news. She was not happy.

I was kind of disappointed myself. A non-meeting meeting would have been fun.

Oh, well, at least I had the beets.

My friends and I did meet that Saturday, at Pizza Express. I should say, *some* of us did. Mary Anne and Claudia each thought the other would be there, so neither of them showed up. Abby didn't look too happy, either. (I think she was still mad at me.)

Over the next two weeks, we saw each other a fair amount. When it was just one or two of us, things were okay. Any more than that, and the squabbling started again.

As for our clients, squabbling was the tip of the iceberg. Some of them were furious. And who did they dump on? Claudia, the Bad News Baby-sitter. Her phone rang constantly that first week, and she must have explained our breakup fifty times.

We knew our charges would be upset, and we all made sure to talk to them and calmly explain that we would still be seeing them. But we weren't prepared for the parents' reactions. Mrs. Arnold practically broke down in tears. Mrs. Wilder wanted to have us over for a counseling session. Mr. Papadakis offered us a "retainer" if we stayed together. (Claudia thought he meant the thing you put on your teeth. He was really talking about a steady weekly payment.)

By the second week, clients started getting the hang of it. They began calling us individually. I got some calls, but I referred them to my friends. I still didn't trust myself after my experience with Jackie. (He, by the way, was recovering very well.)

What did I do with all my free time? Homework, mostly. Gardening, sometimes. Walking Shannon. But one Wednesday I had a great pickup football game with my older brothers and a couple of their neighborhood friends. The Monday after, Watson taught me how to make a killer lasagna.

I still felt the pang on meeting days. But it was fading.

The second Thursday after the breakup, five-thirty passed me right by. I didn't even notice. I was relaxing on the couch, sipping apple cider and trying to do science homework, when the phone rang.

"Crusty, it's for you!" called Sam from the kitchen. (I *hate* that nickname.)

"Thanks, Slime," I called as I ran to the phone.

My eye caught a glimpse of 5:37 on the kitchen clock as I picked up the receiver.

"Hello?"

"Hi, Kristy? It's Claudia." Her voice was a timid whisper. "Can you come over right away?"

"Sure," I said. "Are you okay?"

"Just fabulous," she hissed in an unfabulous way. "I need you right now."

"Sure, Claud. But what — "

"Just come, Kristy! I can't talk. 'Bye."

Uh-oh. Emergency time.

I had to find a ride, and fast.

CHAPTER 9

Name: _Claudia Kishi_

Class: _208_

Date: _Thurz. 9/26_

Our Bodies' Metablism

First you breath and you get some oxyjin and some other elminto that don't efect you to much. They are respired in to youre lungs fill up and somehow gets in to youre blode which goes from blew to red. And youre hart pumps to, with ventricals and auricals. meanwhile their is somting called ~~glizel glizel~~ glyco

Help! Help!! Help!!!!!!

Janine Kishi peered over Claudia's shoulder. "This was your best effort?"

"This stuff is so confusing," Claudia replied.

"What are all these blotches?"

"I was stabbing it with my pen."

"We went over it all, Claudia — respiration, glycolysis, the Krebs cycle, the electron transport chain," Janine said. "You claimed to understand it. From this paper, it doesn't appear you were telling me the truth."

Janine Kishi is the only high school kid I know who sounds like a college professor. She'd been trying to coach Claudia on her science homework. Which is a little like a beaver teaching a basset hound how to build a dam.

"When *you* explain it, I'm even more confused," Claudia complained.

Janine let out a big sigh. "Well, if you'd spend less time on the *phone* . . ."

"What makes you think I was on the phone?"

"I heard you hang up as I was opening the door."

Janine has sharp ears. She'd heard Claudia talking to me.

No, folks, Claudia had not set her kitchen on fire. She had not caught her finger in the Cuisinart. She had not been discovered eating a Ring-Ding by the junk-food police, her parents.

Claudia was in a crisis over her homework.

Had she bothered to tell me that? Noooo. Instead, she had worried me half to death.

Here's what happened after our phone call: I ran through my house to find a ride. Watson was working in his office, behind closed doors. Mom was at work, too, of course, and Nannie had taken Emily to the doctor. Charlie was the only driver left in the family.

I barrelled upstairs and into his room. "Charlie, take me to Claudia's house."

He was sitting with his feet propped up on his desk. He turned to me with a scowl. "Haven't you heard of knocking?"

"She's in trouble," I said. "Something awful has happened."

I ran downstairs and outside to his car. Muttering under his breath, Charlie followed.

Car is a loose description. *Heap of scrap metal* is more like it. It's called the Junk Bucket for a good reason.

I pushed aside a pile of magazines and jumped into the front seat.

As Charlie started the "car" up, he said, "This isn't really a Baby-sitters Club meeting, is it? Because if it is, I expect to be paid."

"No, Charlie, it's not," I replied.

"Great," he grumbled. "So it's just slave labor."

"I don't believe you! One of my best friends may be lying on the floor, gasping for breath, and you're worried about gas money?"

"All right, all right." He started up the Junk Bucket and pulled into the street.

When Charlie dropped me off in front of Claud's house, I ran inside through the front door (which the Kishis leave unlocked) and up to Claudia's room.

She was slumped over her desk. Janine was pacing behind her, arms folded, lecturing her about study habits.

Claudia's face brightened as I walked in.

"Hello, Kristy," Janine said. "I'm sorry, but Claudia is very busy right now — "

"She's coming over to do the homework with me!" Claudia blurted out.

"I am?" I asked.

Claudia shot me a Look.

"I mean, I *am!*" I quickly said.

Janine smirked. "You're so transparent, Kristy. All right, I'll help you both. The Krebs cycle is not exactly an intuitive concept."

"Krebs cycle?" I said. "No problem. I know it like the back of my hand."

I was exaggerating. But I had been studying it. And I kind of understood it. Well, some of it.

"All right," Janine said, walking out of the room with a weary sigh. "When you're running low on collective adenosine triphosphate, don't hesitate to call."

"Right," I said with a smile.

Janine disappeared into her room.

"What'd she say?" Claudia asked.

I shrugged. "How should I know?"

Claudia sank back into her chair. "Kristy, I am $D - E - D$. Dead. I might as well be studying ancient Sanscript."

"Isn't it Sanskrit?" I asked.

"See? I'd flunk that, too."

"Claudia, you had me scared. I thought something awful had happened to you."

"Something awful *has* happened to me — this!" She held out her science textbook, open to a complicated diagram of the heart and lungs. "Explain this, please."

I scanned the diagram, then said, "Okay. First, this is the heart — "

Rrrrrring!

"Arrrrgh! Not again!" Claudia picked up the receiver. "Hello, Claudia Kishi. . . . Hi, Mr. Sobak. I'm sorry, but the Baby-sitters Club has been disbanded. I believe I told your wife . . . That's all right. . . . Yes, we are. . . . Her name is Mary Anne Spier, and you'll have to call her to find out if she's available. . . . She's in the phone book under $S - P -$

E — E — R. No problem. . . . 'Bye."

Claudia slammed down the receiver. "He doesn't listen to his wife, and then, when I go through the trouble to explain everything, he asks for *Mary Anne's* number!"

"It's *S — P — I — E — R*," I said gently.

"*I, E*, what's the difference? I'm doing the best I can. You think it's easy answering all these phone calls? Besides, why should boring old Mary Anne get all the jobs?"

"Claudia!"

"Sorry, sorry, I take it back." Claudia turned her textbook toward me. "Teach me the Crab's Cycle. That'll calm me down."

"Okay, first of all, it's *Krebs*, and it's the way the body makes energy, in the form of ATP — "

"But that's so stupid! Energy isn't a *thing*. It's, like, a state of mind or an attitude — "

Rrrrrring!

With a groan, Claudia reached for the phone. "Hello? . . . Yes, hi, Mrs. Hobart. . . . About two weeks ago. . . . Yes, it's permanent. . . . Well, we're really busy with schoolwork and stuff. . . . It'll be all right. Do you have all our numbers? . . . I know, I'm sorry. . . . A central voice-mail pickup? Well, we can look into it, I guess. . . . Okay, say hi to the boys. 'Bye."

Click.

"What's a central voice-mail pickup?" Claudia asked.

I shrugged. "Beats me. Why don't you just leave your machine on?"

"I tried that. They keep calling back. Then I have to return their calls. It's faster just to answer."

"Okay, well, back to the homework. When you eat, like, a candy bar, your body stores some of it in fat cells, right? But it also — "

Rrrrrring!

"Ohhh, just when we were getting to the good part!" Claudia said.

"I'll take it." I stood up and reached for the phone. "Hello?"

"Hello?" a muffled, high-pitched voice said. "Do you still have the Baby-sitters Club?"

I sat on the director's chair. Claudia was scooting into her closet. "No," I answered, "but we are available individ — "

"No club? Then I'll take the regular baby-sitter's sandwich, one baby-sitter on rye with mayo and a sour pickle."

Now I recognized the voice. "Alan Gray, you are a disgusting goon!" I cried, slamming the phone down.

Claudia emerged from her closet with a bag of Snickers bars. "For scientific demonstration. You know, for the part you were starting to talk about, the candy bar?"

I laughed. Claudia tossed me a bar and plopped onto her bed. We just sat there for a moment, munching happily. I saw my trusty visor buried under some papers on Claudia's floor, so I grabbed it and put it on.

The clock clicked to 5:51. I was in my usual BSC position. Claudia was in hers. We were doing our usual BSC activity, eating.

"Feels like a meeting, huh?" I said.

Claudia nodded. "Kristy, do you miss it?"

I had to take a deep breath. The truth? Right then and there, in Claudia's room, the answer was yes. I couldn't help it.

"Sometimes I do," I replied. "So much that it hurts."

"Me, too," Claudia said sadly. "You know, when I think of all of us, sitting around here, eating stuff — "

"Answering calls — "

"Laughing — "

I smiled. "And arguing."

"Yeah, and changing schedules."

"Listening to excuses."

"Listening to you blow up."

"I *never* blew up!" I boomed.

We both started cracking up. "Well," Claudia said, "I guess I don't miss it *all* the time."

"It does feel good to have the free time," I admitted. "I kind of enjoy spending it at home. It's relaxing."

"I spend it with my homework. That relaxes me so much, I fall asleep. Maybe that's why I'm flunking."

I stood up and walked toward Claud's desk. "Have no fear. You'll pass. That's the Thomas promise."

Claudia took another bite of Snickers. "You know, I can feel a lot of Krebs in my stomach right now. This is helpful."

Rrrrrring!

"Go away!" Claudia shouted. Then she picked up the receiver once again and said politely, "Hello, Claudia Kishi answering service. . . . Uh, actually, she *is* listed, Mr. Sobak. The spelling is *S — P — I — E — R . . .*"

CHAPTER 10

"Use your head, Linny!" shouted Abby.

I heard her voice as I was biking past a field in my neighborhood on a cloudy Saturday, seventeen days ABSC. Abby was playing goal, while a bunch of little kids tried to kick a soccer ball in her direction.

Linny looked totally confused.

"If the ball's too high to kick, you can butt it with your head," Abby explained.

"Cool!" Linny began charging around with his head down, like a goat. "Yo!" he shouted. "Kick it to me!"

He butted a six-year-old boy named Timmy Hsu, who turned around and jumped on nine-year-old Linny's back. Sheila Nofziger, who lives down the block, sat on the ball and began bouncing. Scott Hsu, Hannie Papadakis, and Moon Pinckney were kicking around an empty soda can. (Sheila, Scott, Hannie, and Moon are all seven.)

100

I supposed it was a soccer practice. To me, it looked more like pandemonium.

Abby was cracking up. As if the fundamentals of the game meant nothing.

That's what separates Abby from me. She's a natural athlete. I'm a sportsperson. The difference? Dedication and discipline. (I'm not being conceited. It's just a fact.)

Not long before, I'd been pretty annoyed at Abby. I know the feeling was mutual, because Abby hadn't sat with me on the bus for weeks.

I felt bad about that. Enough was enough. We'd disagreed over BSC-related stuff. Now that the club was defunct, what was the point of staying angry?

She needed help coaching. And the kids needed real guidance.

I just had to stop.

Abby's back was to me as I climbed off my bike and unstrapped my helmet. I flipped down my kickstand and walked toward the field.

"Hi!" I called out. "Can I help out?"

Abby spun around. "Heyyy, guys, time to get serious! It's World Cup Kristy!"

"Who wants to play a real game?" I announced.

"Meeeeeee!" the kids answered.

"It's Kristy's Kickers versus Abby's Attackers!" Abby announced.

We chose sides. Abby and I decided we'd play the field and help the kids. Hannie was goalie for the Kickers, Sheila for the Attackers.

The Kickers won the coin toss. I took the ball and dribbled in. "Now watch how I keep the ball in front of me," I said. "Soft kicks, each one closer to the goal — "

Suddenly the ball was gone. Abby was racing down the field with it, whooping at the top of her lungs.

She passed it to Scott. Scott kicked it past Hannie, who happened to be busy picking her nose.

"Score!" Scott shouted.

"Yeaaaa!" yelled his teammates.

"No fair!" Hannie protested.

Abby was giggling. I was not amused. "Uh, you know," I said, "this is a practice game. We're supposed to be showing them fundamentals."

"Stealing the ball is fundamental," said Abby. "But, hey, if you want me to take it easy on you, I will."

Ooooh. That was low. If Abby wanted competition, competition she'd get.

"Time out!" I shouted. "Kickers, team meeting!"

I assigned positions. We discussed strategy. I gave my team a huge pep talk.

We ran onto the field, pumped up and ready.

How was our game? In a word, atrocious.

Scott Hsu kneed his brother in the nose. Another Kicker, Kyle Abou-Sabh, booted the ball into the wrong goal. Moon kicked off a sneaker and it flew into a nearby Dumpster. Abby stole the ball from me three more times.

The Attackers won, 17–6.

"Great game!" Abby put her arm around me as we packed up to leave. "Don't worry. I'll let you win next time."

"*Whaaaat!*"

She ran off, giggling. I was about to chase after her when Hannie Papadakis tugged at my sleeve.

"Kristy, my daddy makes houses and stuff," she said.

"Yes, Hannie," I replied. "I know that — "

"So, like, he could build you a new clubhouse. You know, for the one that broke."

I had no idea what she was talking about. "I don't have a broken clubhouse."

"My mom told me there's no more Baby-sitters Club," Hannie explained.

"Oh, that means we're not meeting anymore. Our clubhouse was Claudia's bedroom. It's still there."

Hannie looked confused. "So why can't you meet?"

Linny came bounding over. "Because they don't like each other anymore, silly."

"That's not true!" The words flew out of my mouth, even though I wasn't sure I believed them. Abby had been really competitive — *too* competitive.

"Then why is Abby running away from you?" Timmy asked.

"Look," I said. "All us baby-sitters are still friends. We don't have formal meetings anymore, that's all. But we still sit."

"Yyyyess!" Timmy exclaimed.

"Can you sit for us?" Hannie asked.

"Us, too!" Moon and Sheila shouted.

Abby walked up behind them. "Hrrrmph. How about me?"

Scott looked at her blankly. "You're too old to have a baby-sitter."

"I *am* a baby-sitter!" Abby retorted.

"Yeah? Cool!" Scott said.

By then the other kids were beginning to scamper home. Scott took off after them.

Abby and I called out good-byes, then walked to our bikes. "I guess you haven't sat for the Hsus yet, huh?" I asked.

"Or Sheila, or Moon, or a lot of the BSC clients." Abby sighed. "I was starting to know some of them. But since the BSC broke up, forget it. Their parents don't ever think to call me."

104

"I know Claudia gives out your phone number."

Abby mounted her bike. "I was the newest member, Kristy. Everyone knows you guys much better."

"Well, let's do something about it," I said as we began riding home. "You know, make some phone calls, ask some parents to give references — "

"Nahh, it's all right. I don't mind. I mean, it's kind of relaxing not to have to baby-sit. I can do homework, listen to Anna practice, take naps, watch the leaves turn, clean the bathrooms."

I gave her a Look. She gave me a Look.

"Aggggh! Bring back the BSC!" she shouted.

I felt my heart jump. The pang was back again. She couldn't really mean that, could she? Was she right? Was everyone feeling this way?

Easy, Kristy, I told myself. Haven't you been through this a million times already?

Abby had this exaggerated, mock-hysterical expression on her face. She was kidding. A typical Abby joke.

As we left the field and turned onto the street, I stood up, began pushing hard, and yelled, "Race!"

"No fair!" Abby called out behind me.

Not true. I let her pull ahead even before I started trying.

Then I really let her have it. I raced along, tearing around McLelland with an easy lead.

I would have pulled right up my driveway if a car weren't blocking it.

It was one of the Pikes' station wagons. My mom was chatting with Mrs. Pike by the driver's side. David Michael was waiting for Nicky Pike to climb out the back door.

I glided to a stop behind them. "Hi!"

Behind me, Abby whooshed by, heading toward her house. "Race isn't over yet!" she called out.

I ignored her. (No one had said we were racing to *her* house.) "Hi, Kristy!" Mrs. Pike said.

"How's Mallory?" I asked.

She shook her head sadly. "I don't know what's gotten into her. She's home working, on a Saturday. It's for some library reading group. She's writing about the influence of Marguerite Henry on the *Saddle Club*, or something like that." She sighed and winked at my mom. "I tried to convince her to go outside, but uh-uh, no way."

I nodded. "I guess Mal's not upset about the BSC breakup anymore, huh?"

Mrs. Pike shrugged. "She hasn't talked about it much."

106

"Great. Well, say hi from me."

Hasn't talked about it much? The words hit me in a strange way.

I knew I should have been happy. But part of me wished they were still upset. Part of me wished *someone* would sincerely beg me to start the BSC again. Even though I'd say no.

I mean, was the BSC that easy to forget? Was it that small a part of everyone's life? After all that time, all that effort?

I thought of something I'd never considered before.

Maybe my great idea had never been so great in the first place.

CHAPTER 11

"I thought she was dying!" said Erica Blumberg as she shoved part of her lunch in her mouth. "Shushuf quy um quy — "

Across the lunch table, Lily Karp remarked, "Very tasteful, Erica. Will you swallow, please?"

Erica gulped and kept right on talking. "She was crying and crying. First I thought she had gas, so I tried to burp her. Then I thought she needed a nap, so I put her in her crib and turned on her electric mobile and stuff. She just cried louder. So then I thought, like, whoa, something was seriously wrong. Should I call the doctor or nine-one-one or what? I was going crazy!"

"So what happened?" Lily asked.

"It was her diaper! Can you believe it? Totally soaked. I mean, *duh*. I hadn't changed her all day!"

Duh was right. Any half-brained baby-sitter

would have checked the diaper in the first place.

Yes, I was eavesdropping. I couldn't help it. Erica and Lily were sitting at the table right behind me. They were talking about a sitting job with the Newtons. This bothered me a lot.

Why? Because the Newtons have always been loyal BSC clients. And because their baby, Lucy, deserves better treatment than Erica had given her.

You know what else? Erica had mentioned her fee. It was a whole dollar more per hour than the BSC charged. That didn't help my mood one bit.

"I know what you mean," Lily continued. "The diapers absorb all the moisture. How are you supposed to know?"

I could keep my mouth shut no longer. I pushed aside my turkey burger and spun around to face them. "When it's lumpy."

"Huh?" Lily asked.

"When the diaper's really wet, the absorbent material becomes lumpy," I explained. "Heavy, too. Did you ever see a kid with diapers come out of a swimming pool?"

From Erica's expression, you'd think my nose had just sprouted celery.

"The diaper swells up," I went on. "The kid looks like the Sta-Puf marshmallow man. That's how absorbent that stuff is. After awhile it becomes really uncomfortable and the baby can develop a rash, so you have to check constantly."

"I definitely waited too long," Erica said. "But I put Vaseline on the rash."

"That works okay, but it stains clothes," I replied. "You're better off with Desitin or something else that has zinc oxide."

Lily laughed. "How do you know this stuff?"

"Experience," I replied. "All that time in the Baby-sitters Club."

"Cool," Lily said. "Now some of us will finally have a chance to learn."

I must have given her a Look, because her face fell. "I didn't mean that in a bad way," she went on. "It's just that, you know, parents never used to call us."

"Mrs. Newton said she tried a bunch of Baby-sitters Club members before she called me." Erica lifted an eyebrow. "Boy, did that make me feel special."

"You did have kind of a monopoly, Kristy," Lily added.

"Oh, come on," I said. "You mean to tell me you *never* baby-sat while the BSC was together?"

Erica shook her head. "How could I? The Newtons live in my neighborhood, plus the

Perkinses and Hobarts — all Baby-sitters Club clients."

"I sat three times last year," Lily volunteered, "for my cousins."

By now the cafeteria was filling up. A group of girls set their trays down opposite Erica and Lily.

"Anyway," Erica said, "it was nice of you to give me all that advice. Thanks."

"You're welcome," I replied, turning back to my meal.

Monopoly?

The word was throbbing in my mind, like a blinking neon light. The BSC had been many things to me. A club. A business. A fun time. A learning experience. But a monopoly? I had never thought of that. Our goal was to be good sitters, not to be the only sitters in town.

No wonder Erica was so incompetent. She hadn't had a chance.

All because of us. The Baby-sitting Hogs.

Stacey sat across from me with her lunch tray. "Thirty cents for your thoughts."

"Thirty cents?" I asked.

"That's the change I got from lunch." Stacey smiled. "Speak."

"Stacey, I just thought of a great idea."

"Uh-oh. Should I eat before I listen to this?"

"An advice service," I continued. "Tips on

baby-sitting, for kids who are new to the business. First we ask Claudia to make a flier. Then we post them all over the school, the recreation center, supermarkets . . ."

As I barrelled on, Stacey's smile slowly disappeared.

Well, I didn't have any more luck with my new idea. Mary Anne had the nicest reaction. She said it might work better on an informal basis. Abby said I should do the service alone, so she could call me. Claudia just laughed.

I wasn't too insulted. I mean, after what happened at Jackie's, who was I to be giving out advice about baby-sitting?

After school that day, I took David Michael and Linny and Hannie Papadakis to the neighborhood field for a *real* soccer practice. It was warm and summery outside, and I started thinking about how stuffy it would feel if I were in Claudia's room, sweating out a meeting. Then I remembered Claudia's air conditioner, and the great lemonade she used to serve . . .

Arrgh! Keep your mind on the practice, Thomas.

We were in the middle of a three-on-two drill when I heard a shout from the sidewalk.

"Can I play?"

Scott Hsu was running across the grass toward me.

"Heyyyy, Scott!" I called out. "Of course you can! Where is — "

Before the words left my mouth, I saw my answer. Timmy was walking up the sidewalk with Cokie Mason.

My heart did a cannonball dive. I blinked my eyes, just in case I was seeing things.

"Is that . . . your sitter?" I asked Scott.

But Scott was already off kicking the ball around.

"Scott!" Cokie called out. "*SCOTT HSU, GET OVER HERE THIS INSTANT!*"

Well, that was Cokie's style. If a cologne were based on Cokie, it would be called Obnoxious. Never in my wildest dreams had I ever put together the concepts *Cokie* and *babysitter*.

"Oh, come on," Scott pleaded.

"*You heard me!*" Cokie snapped. "*I need to get to the store now!*"

Scott shoved his hands in his pockets and trudged angrily off the field.

I was not going to take this lightly. I followed him. "Hey, Cokie?" I said as politely as I could. "I'll look after him."

Timmy lit up. "Me, too!" he shouted.

"Ugh, did you have to say that?" Cokie

hissed through tight lips. "Look, today is the last day of the pre-inventory sale at Bellair's. If I don't go there now, I'll never find anything."

"You're taking them on a shopping trip for yourself?" I asked. ("Selfish pig," I didn't say.)

"Yeah. So?"

"Well, why not leave them here? You'll have time to yourself, and you can pick them up on the way back."

"Yeah!" Timmy shrieked. "Can we? Can we?"

Cokie's lips curled in disgust. "I'm their baby-sitter, Kristin, not you." She grabbed the boys by their hands and started walking. "Get a life."

I nearly pummelled her. Really. If I hadn't been surrounded by kids, if I hadn't needed to set an example, she'd have been history.

The poor Hsu kids shuffled down the road with her, like captured stray puppies on the way to the pound.

The rest of the practice? The kids loved it. They ran all over me. I was so angry and spaced out, thinking about Cokie, that I could barely pay attention.

Later that evening I called the Hsus.

"Hi, Kristy, long time no hear!" Mrs. Hsu said. "How's life after the Baby-sitters Club?"

"Fine," I replied. "Um, guess who I saw?

Scott and Timmy, with Cokie. As we were chatting I said to myself, 'Kristy, maybe you never mentioned to Mrs. Hsu that the members of the club are all available for sitting at our home numbers.' "

Mrs. Hsu laughed. "You did, Kristy. Several times. So did Claudia and Stacey. And I'm sure I'll use you. It's just that Mrs. Mason is a good friend, and she's been after me for the longest time to give her daughter a sitting job. I always meant to, but the Baby-sitters Club was so convenient and reliable. Now that you're all scattered, I figured, why not give Cokie a chance?"

"Sure, I understand," I said. "Well, nice to talk to you. And don't stop calling on us former BSC members!"

"I won't. 'Bye."

Boy, was I cheery. My voice had not one drop of bitterness in it.

I didn't start screaming bloody murder until I hung up the phone.

CHAPTER 12

PRIVATE JOURNAL
ANASTASIA McGILL

Saturday
I feel awful today. It all came rushing back.

I thought I'd recovered. I thought I'd finally felt one hundred percent fine about the BSC split-up.

But I was wrong. Funny how some things have a way of creeping up on you in the strangest places. . .

I could count on the fingers of no hands the number of times Stacey had shown me her private journal. This time, she said, was an exception. It felt to her like a BSC notebook entry.

On Saturday morning, she and Claudia were at Washington Mall. They were cleaning out Steven E, the mall's fanciest store, which was having a clearance sale.

Stacey loves sales. She marks them on her calendar in advance. She prepares for them by going to bed early the night before. Her motto is "Maximum Fashion for Maximum Savings."

Personally, I think the idea is ridiculous. Take the "Savings" part. You don't *save* money in a sale. You spend it. (Don't even ask me my opinion of "Fashion.")

"We should have brought a shopping cart," Stacey said as they trudged through the atrium with their Steven E bags.

Claudia groaned. "My parents are going to kill me."

"Don't worry. They know a bargain when they see it. Just have them feel the fabric of the black silk blouse."

"A college scholarship — *that's* a bargain to them. A library book sale. Home delivery of *The Wall Street Journal*. But this? Honestly, Stacey, when my dad sees his credit card he'll

117

make me pay him back in installments until I'm twenty-nine."

"We can return some of it," Stacey suggested.

Claudia stopped walking. She and Stacey looked back at the store.

"Nahhhh," they said together.

Claudia headed straight for the elevator. "Come on, let's eat."

They rode up to the food court and stood in line at Friendly's.

Through the din of the crowded restaurant, Claudia heard a crash and a baby's loud squawk.

A waitress ran by with a hand broom and dustpan, dodging her way through the room. She began cleaning up the floor near a booth in the corner. Claud could see Mrs. Newton crouching over to help out. Jamie was watching with a guilty expression while Lucy gurgled in her high chair.

Stacey smiled. "Oops."

"Right this way!" a waiter called out. He led Stacey and Claudia to a table in the back of the restaurant.

Stacey put her bag under her chair. "Order me plain broiled chicken and a green salad with dressing on the side. I'll be right back."

The floor near the Newtons' booth was spotless now. Stacey snuck up quietly, keeping herself out of view behind the high-backed seat. Jamie, who's four, was slurping spaghetti, his back turned to her. She gently placed her hands over his eyes. "Guess who?"

Mrs. Newton winked and nodded hello. Lucy drooled.

Jamie said, "Laverne?"

"Who's Laverne?" Stacey asked.

"The waitress," Jamie replied.

"Nnnngeeee!" Lucy squealed.

"Wrong again." Stacey pulled her hands away. "Surprise!"

When Jamie saw her, he scowled. Before Stacey could react, he slipped out of his seat and walked away.

"Jamie?" Mrs. Newton called out. "Where are you going?"

"I'll bring him back," Stacey volunteered.

She turned and gave Claudia the one-finger *I'll-be-with-you-in-a-minute* signal. Then she took off.

Jamie headed toward the gumball machines near the door. But just as Stacey caught up to him, he scampered off again.

"Ohhhh, playing hard-to-get?" Stacey said.

Jamie nearly plowed into a busboy, who was carrying a full tray. He headed straight into the men's room, pulling the door closed behind him.

Stacey stood outside the bathroom and knocked. "It's me."

"You can't come in!" he shouted through the closed door. "It's for boys and men!"

"I know. I'll wait."

Well, she waited. And waited.

Finally an old man walked up and pulled the door open. Jamie came flying out, his hand still tightly clutching the handle.

"Sorry, young fel — " the man began.

But Jamie was off again.

This time Stacey was able to follow close behind. She grabbed onto him and wrapped him in a big hug. "Got you!"

Jamie's arms were flailing. "Let me go!"

"Okay, okay," Stacey said, setting him down. "I was only joking."

They were by the cashier now, in a corner safely away from the restaurant traffic. Jamie's eyes were welling up. He wouldn't look at Stacey.

"Wow, you're in some mood," Stacey said. "What's up?"

"Nothing," he murmured.

"Did I say something wrong?"

"I want my mom."

"Sure, Jamie." Now Stacey was totally bewildered. She walked him back to the booth. He slid into the padded seat and shrunk into a corner.

120

"See, sweetheart, Stacey doesn't hate you," Mrs. Newton said.

"Hate you?" Stacey repeated. "Of course not. Why would I?"

Mrs. Newton looked up at Stacey with a weary smile. "I hired Erica Blumberg to sit a couple of times. I didn't realize how that would affect Jamie. I mean, she's a perfectly nice girl, but Jamie is used to the Baby-sitters Club. I tried to explain what had happened, but somehow he's convinced himself that you all hate him."

Stacey sidled into the seat next to Jamie. "That sure isn't true. We still adore you."

"Yeah?" Jamie said. "Then why is smelly Erica our sitter?"

"I told you, honey," Mrs. Newton said to Jamie, "I won't always be able to reach the same sitters as I used to. They're not a club anymore."

"Why not?" Jamie demanded.

"Well," Stacey said, "it's just that we all had a lot of other personal commitments and schoolwork, and we couldn't keep our meeting times."

Stacey felt foolish saying that. Jamie just looked at her as if she were speaking a foreign language.

Claudia eventually came over, lugging the two shopping bags, and *she* tried to console Jamie.

"Jamie," Mrs. Newton finally said, "I promise, I'll hire Stacey or Claudia to sit for you next time. And they'll come. Right, girls?"

"Right," Claudia and Stacey said.

Jamie grumbled an "Okay," but he still didn't seem happy.

By that time Lucy was restless, so the Newtons had to leave. Stacey and Claudia returned to their lukewarm lunches.

The glamour had gone out of the shopping trip.

Mr. Kishi picked them up soon afterward. His reaction to Claudia's purchases? Well, let's just say no one was singing on the ride home.

As soon as she was dropped off, Stacey ran inside. "Mo-o-o-om, come see what I — "

Her mother poked her head out of the kitchen. "Stacey, call Mrs. Prezzioso right away. She needs a sitter for tonight. Here's the number."

Stacey put down her bags and took a sheet of notepaper from her mom's outstretched hand. "Thanks."

She ran into the living room, sat on the sofa, and tapped out the Prezziosos' number.

"Hello?" said Mrs. P.

"Hi, it's Stacey! Listen, I'm sorry I wasn't here but I can do the job — "

"You know, dear," Mrs. P. interrupted, "I spent the whole morning on the phone. I did manage to reach Mary Anne, however, so I'm covered. But thanks for calling back."

"You're welcome," Stacey replied, feeling a little deflated. "Say hi to Mary Anne."

"Stacey, I hope you don't mind my saying this," Mrs. P. went on, "but this whole process was much easier when you were the Baby-sitters Club."

Stacey let out a sigh. "I know, Mrs. P. Believe me, I know."

CHAPTER 13

"Twenty-four . . . thirty-eight . . . nineteen . . .

I, Quarterback Kristy, was waiting for the right moment to begin my pass play. My center, Charlie, was hunched in front of me, ready to snap the ball on command.

Honnnk! Honnnk! a car sounded from the street.

"Seventy-three . . . eight hundred and five . . ."

Our opposing team, David Michael and Sam, were starting to sag. "*Bo*-ring," Sam called out.

That was my moment.

"Hike!" I yelled.

Honnnnnnk! went the car.

Charlie snapped the football to me and took off across our backyard like a shot.

I had our adversaries where I wanted them. Off balance. Lost in Duh-land.

I dropped back and passed. The ball spiraled toward Charlie's waiting hands.

HONNNK!

Charlie dropped the ball.

"Arrrgh!" he cried out. "Who is that — "

Suddenly Stacey ran into the backyard. "Kristy, come quickly. Jackie's in the hospital!"

So much for the game. I was off and running. "Tell Mom where I went!" I shouted over my shoulder.

Racing after Stacey, I called out, "What happened?"

"He fell off his bike and hurt his head," Stacey yelled back.

Mrs. McGill's car was idling at the curb. Abby was already sitting in the front seat. (She lives two houses away, so I guess the first few horn blasts had been for her.) Stacey and I jumped in the backseat and slammed the door.

As we pulled away from the curb, I asked, "Is he badly hurt?"

"Charlotte wasn't sure," Stacey replied. "She was the one who called to tell me. Her mom's on duty in the emergency room. She managed to admit him right into a regular hospital room."

"Was he wearing his helmet?" Abby asked.

"Nope," Stacey replied.

I groaned. "I always *tell* him to!"

Stacey shrugged. "That's Jackie."

I could barely breathe as we sped along. Stacey's eyes were misty. Abby was staring grimly out the window.

Before long Mrs. McGill was swerving into the Stoneybrook General Hospital parking lot. She found a space near the emergency room, and we all raced inside.

"Rodowsky!" I said to the receptionist.

She raised her eyebrows and pointed to the left. "Follow the crowd."

Down the hallway, Mary Anne, Mallory, Jessi, and Claudia were gathered outside Jackie's room.

We called hellos, and I peeked in.

Jackie was on a bed, propped almost upright, clutching an enormous stuffed bear. His mom, dad, Shea, and Archie sat on the other side of the bed, looking worried.

"Hi, Jackie!" I called out.

"Kristy!" Jackie turned and tried to climb out of bed.

Nine pairs of arms reached out to prevent another accident.

"Adverb," Shea called out, reading from a Mad Libs booklet.

"What's a adverb?" Archie asked.

Shea sighed wearily. "It's a verb from an advertisement, like brush teeth or eat Wheaties."

While a bunch of grammar volunteers tried to set Shea straight, I knelt down near Jackie. "I didn't have time to buy flowers."

He smiled. "I hate flowers. Did you bring chocolate?"

"Oops, next time," I replied. "How did this happen, big guy?"

Jackie looked embarrassed. "Well, um, you know that really steep hill just around the corner from your house?"

"Sure. What were you doing so far from *your* house?"

"Falling off my bike. I went too fast, and a car was coming the other way, and I got scared, and I kind of ran into a tree and fell. Now I have a combustion."

"Concussion," Shea the wordsmith corrected him.

"They have to drain some stuff from my skull," Jackie continued.

"Fluid," Shea elaborated.

I must have looked really worried, because Mrs. Rodowsky leaned over the bed and grasped me reassuringly by the arm. "He's going to be okay. He just has to lie still for a few days and stay under observation."

Jackie nodded. "I was unconscience — "

"*Scious*," Shea interjected.

"Gesundheit," Abby said.

"And when I woke up," Jackie went on,

"the hospital guys were putting me in an ambulance and all these people were watching. I didn't know any of them. It was scary. All I was trying to do was bike to your house and give you that." He pointed to a wadded-up pile of tissues, Band-Aids, dollar bills, lint, and scraps of paper.

"Which part of it?" I asked.

"The yellow piece of paper."

I reached into the pile, pulled out a folded note, and read it:

> deer kristy,
>   I did'nt meen to fall out of the tree. I was only kiding. And I lernd my lessin so Il'l never do it agan. So dont be mad. Tell all the babby siters what I said OK? Maybe they won't be mad ether so they can be a club again.
>   From,
>   your frend
>   WHACKY JACKIE

I had to read it twice before I had the slightest idea what he meant. "Jackie," I said, "you don't think *you* were the reason the BSC split up, do you?"

"I'm really really really sorry," Jackie replied. "I was being stupid. I didn't mean to make you mad. Really."

Abby took the note out of my hand. As she

read it, my other friends looked over her shoulder.

"Jackie, that was my fault," I said. "I was your sitter. I should have been looking after you — "

"I mean, I know I'm, like, this big klutz and all," Jackie continued. "But I can be better. Sometimes I do dumb stuff just to be funny, and — "

"Jackie, you can't blame yourself for everything," I said. "You're a kid. All kids make mistakes. I mean, sure, you make me mad sometimes. Especially when you don't listen. I'm mad that you weren't wearing your helmet. But I'm much, much more happy that you're well. And that time you fell out of the tree? It had absolutely, totally nothing to do with the BSC breakup."

"Zero," Abby agreed.

"Zilch," Claudia added.

"*Nada*," Jessi said.

"Pronoun," Shea called out.

"We really love you, Jackie," I said. "Exactly the way you are, bruises and all."

I could see tears forming in Jackie's eyes. Behind me, Mary Anne was sniffling away.

One by one, we leaned into Jackie and gave him kisses.

"Yuck!" Archie yelled.

"Come on!" Shea said. "Pronoun! Like the

New York Knicks. A name of a pro team!"

We all started cracking up.

I looked around the room. "Do you realize," I said softly to Mary Anne, "this is the first time we've all been in the same room since the breakup?"

"Uh . . . huh." Mary Anne could hardly answer. I didn't know if she was choked up about the BSC or Jackie.

To tell you the truth, I was almost a little misty-eyed myself.

"I have tissues!" Jackie reached around to his bed table. His arm brushed against a plastic cup filled with water.

It teetered. I reached out to catch it.

With a dull splash, it hit the floor.

"Jackieeeee," his mom groaned.

I tried as hard as I could not to laugh.

Jackie was going to be just fine. I knew it.

At least as long as he was in the hospital.

CHAPTER 14

"Eighteen," Mallory and I called out together, "nineteen . . . twenty! Ready or not — "

"No! Count to a hundred!" Claire Pike cried from somewhere in the house.

Mal and I exchanged a look. "We'll compromise," I said. "Twenty-five."

We turned back to the fireplace and started to complete the countdown.

When we reached twenty-three, Claire screamed, "Ready!"

Mallory and I took off.

Have you ever played hide-and-seek with seven little kids? It isn't easy. But that's life in the Pike house.

Claire is Mallory's youngest sibling. She's five. The others are Margo (seven); Nicky (eight); Vanessa (nine); and Byron, Jordan, and Adam, who are the ten-year-old triplets.

I hadn't wanted to take this sitting job. I

hadn't lost the fear of sitting I'd developed after Jackie's tree accident. But seeing Jackie the day before had helped. And Mal had called me personally.

Besides, I kind of missed the Pike tribe.

As we walked into the dining room, I spotted a pair of sneakers sticking out from under a floor-to-ceiling window curtain. "I think we need more light in here," I said, pulling the curtains aside to reveal Adam. "Gotcha!"

"No fair!" he yelled. "You saw me!"

"That's what they're supposed to do, doofus!" called a voice from under the piano.

"I found Byron!" Mallory said.

"Ha! Who's the doofus?" Adam crowed.

Vanessa was next. I found her hiding in the bathtub.

"Figures," Adam said. "That's her favorite room."

"I am rubber, you are glue . . ." Vanessa began chanting.

"Vanessa's in the bathroom, p. u.!" Byron finished.

As the three of them went off chasing each other, Mallory and I made more discoveries: Margo under her parents' bed, Nicky behind the loose pillows on the family room sofa, and Jordan behind a refrigerator box in the basement.

That still left Claire.

After a thorough basement search, we walked upstairs. "I'll take the second floor," I said.

Mallory nudged me in the ribs and pointed toward the open door of the family room.

Through it, I could see an inner closet door creaking out a bit.

Mallory scampered into the room, saying, "Gee, Kristy, I'll bet she went outside. Let's grab some coats and — "

As she pulled open the closet door, Claire shrieked with delight.

"There you are!" Mallory exclaimed. "What a great hiding place!"

"Say you can't find me," Claire whispered excitedly. "Tell Adam and Vanessa and them to look."

"Okay," Mal replied. She turned away, closing the door behind her.

"AAAAAAAAAA!"

That was not a shriek of delight. Mallory and I whirled around. I yanked the closet door open again.

Claire was clutching her left index finger, screaming. Her eyes were popping, her face bright red.

"Oh no oh no oh no!" Mallory cried, picking up Claire and racing her to the bathroom.

The other Pikes were now thundering toward us. "What happened?" Adam yelled.

I ran into the kitchen to fetch an ice pack from the freezer.

When I returned, Mallory was holding Claire's finger under cold water.

"You closed the door on my finger!" Claire wailed.

Mallory was sobbing. "I'm sorry, I'm sorry, I'm sorry."

"AAAAAAAAAA!"

Poor Claire. I'd never heard her scream so loudly. Her brothers and sisters stood there in shock. Margo was all teary-eyed herself, in sympathy.

I took Claire's hand and applied the ice pack. "Call the doctor," I told Mallory.

A few moments later she returned, wiping away tears. "The doctor says that if Claire can move the finger, probably nothing's broken. But we should take her in anyway, just as soon as Mom and Dad come home."

I held Claire for about five minutes. By that time her shrieks had quieted to whimpers. Her fingertip was red but not swollen.

I took the ice pack away and Claire slowly moved her finger.

"How does it feel now?" I asked.

"Better," Claire mumbled.

Her brothers and sisters were now wandering away. But Mallory was standing in the bathroom doorway, her head hung low. "Sorry, Claire," she repeated.

"It really really hurt," was Claire's response. Taking her ice pack, she walked out of the bathroom and into the family room.

Mallory and I hung out in the hallway, silently keeping an eye on the kids. They all gathered around Claire, who held up her finger proudly like a trophy.

In a soft, angry voice, Mallory said, "That was so, so stupid of me. How could I have closed the door while she was in there?"

"Mal, it was an accident," I said. "You couldn't see where her finger was."

"Some baby-sitter. I end up sending my own sister to the doctor."

"Look, Mal. A bad sitter neglects. A bad sitter does selfish things. You're a great sitter. You were just playing. Everything you did was careful. Stuff like this just happens."

"I guess," Mallory said.

We heard a car pulling into the driveway. The entire pack of kids barged out of the family room and ran outside. I tagged close behind.

Mallory carefully explained to Mr. and Mrs. Pike what had happened. Claire tried hard to cry, but it didn't really work.

Mrs. Pike gave Claire a hug and said, "Mallory, I did the same thing to you when you were three. Only it was your bedroom door. Do you remember?"

Mal shook her head.

"We'll just have to do for Claire what we did for you," Mr. Pike continued.

Claire looked terrified. "Am I going to have a shot?"

"Nope," her father replied. "A trip to the doctor, and then a stop at the ice-cream store. Who wants to come?"

"*MEEEEEEEEE!*" shouted every last Pike.

I held myself back. I waved good-bye as they left. I fetched my bike from the backyard and rode home (with my helmet on).

I was very, very lucky to find a full pint of Häagen-Dazs chocolate chocolate chip in my fridge.

As I devoured it, I noticed this funny feeling in my gut.

No, it wasn't the ice cream. I was thinking about my job with the Pikes and my visit with Jackie at the hospital.

Mallory was so wrong to take the blame for Claire's finger. Jackie was so wrong to take the blame for the BSC breakup.

And for the first time, I began realizing I'd been wrong, too. Way wrong.

Jackie's fall from the tree had been haunting

me. Making me feel like a rotten, irresponsible sitter.

I had warned him. I had forbidden him to climb. What else could I have done? Put him on a leash? Coated the tree with Vaseline so he couldn't climb?

I had done the best I could. That was all a baby-sitter could do.

Everything you did was careful. Stuff like this just happens. Those were the words I'd said to Mallory. I might as well have been talking to myself.

I looked at my reflection in the stainless steel serving bowl on the kitchen table. Pushing my baseball hat low over my eyes, I said, "You're good, kid," out of the side of my mouth, like an old-movie gangster.

I cracked up. I felt so goony.

But it was true. I *was* a good sitter.

A good sitter who enjoyed her work. Who loved kids.

Memories of the Baby-sitters Club began to flood in. Of crazy weekend events. Of laughing so hard at meetings that I thought I'd gag.

We were all good sitters. Each of us.

Together, we were great. Too bad the club hadn't worked out.

As I shoved a spoonful of ice cream into my mouth, my eyes kind of welled up.

It was my fault, really. I could have figured out a way to avoid the breakup. I'd been so upset over Jackie, I couldn't think straight. When the BSC faced a major problem, what did I do?

I gave up. Suggested we disband.

That was my idea. Me, Kristy the Problem Tamer.

What had happened since then? Was life so much better now? Was the freedom really worth it?

I wasn't seeing my best friends nearly as much as I used to. Claudia and Mary Anne were still locked in a feud, which might be over if we were a group that talked things out. Stoneybrook parents were in the same situation they'd been in before the BSC — only worse, because they weren't used to it.

Maybe forming the Baby-sitters Club hadn't been my worst idea ever.

Maybe breaking it up was.

My swirling, jumbled mind was settling down. I was seeing things clearly now. I knew exactly what had to be done.

I wanted us to try it again. The right way. Listening. Talking. Doing whatever would be necessary to make the group successful.

No. Successful *and* happy.

The BSC deserved another chance.

I took a deep breath. Way back when I'd first thought up the BSC, I knew I had to do one important thing right away.

I felt the same way now.

I picked up the phone. Taking a deep breath, I tapped out Mary Anne's number.

CHAPTER 15

"Order!" I announced.

It was 5:30. Claud's room was full. One hundred percent attendance, even Shannon and Logan. I'd called them all, and they'd come. That was a good sign. At least they were interested.

"Hrrrmph." I was determined not to say anything stupid, so I'd prepared a statement. Unfolding it, I carefully read: " 'I have called this meeting to discuss the progress of the absence of the Baby-sitters Club and its effect on the future of the members in general and the greater baby-sitting community at large including clients past and possibly future, pending the outcome of this meeting.' "

They all stared at me.

"Is this multiple choice or essay?" Logan asked.

I threw a candy wrapper at him. "Very funny."

"Could you try it again," Abby said, "only slower, as if we're learning English for the first time?"

I dropped my sheet. "Okay. I don't know about you guys, but I really miss baby-sitting."

Claudia exhaled loudly. "Uh-oh."

"We still baby-sit, Kristy," Stacey remarked.

"I know we do, but things are so different."

"Waaaiiit a minute," Logan said. "Am I hearing right? Are you saying we should get back together? You, Kristy Thomas of 'Kristy's Sitting Service'? As in 'That's what we're becoming, anyway'?"

"Logannnn," Mary Anne chided him.

"That's what she said," Logan reminded her.

"I agree with Kristy," Mallory said. "The last few weeks have been no fun."

"I . . . I second!" Jessi blurted out, all excited. "Oh, I can't believe this. Mme Noelle — the Friday schedule isn't — I mean, the families go away — "

"Uh, Jessi?" Abby said. "Words in put sentences right way the together please?"

Jessi gulped, then spoke slowly: "A lot of the kids in ballet class are having trouble with the Friday schedule, because their parents like to go away early on weekend family trips. Mme Noelle figured it would only become

141

worse during snow season, so she wants to reschedule lessons to Tuesday!"

"Yyyyes!" I exclaimed.

"And my creative writing group is ending in three weeks," Mallory added.

"Excellent," I said. "We can be a little flexible about that. I mean, you're already in it."

"I am not hearing this," Claudia muttered.

"Look, guys, let's think before we jump into anything," Stacey said. "We can't just form the club again, wave a magic wand, and expect everything to be perfect. How do you know we won't come up against the same problems again?"

"Like what, needing more free time?" Abby asked. "Ha! I sure have enjoyed that. I spent all Saturday watching the chrome rust on my mom's car. Which was almost as much fun as waiting for the bananas to turn brown in the kitchen. At least *you* all have had a few jobs. I'm not sitting at all. No one calls me."

"Yeah? Then I should get call forwarding," Claudia remarked. "I could send clients to you. They think they can call me twenty-four hours a day. The last time Mr. Hobart called, I made him help me with my math homework."

"It hasn't been so great for the rest of us, Abby," Mary Anne said. "The clients are calling other sitters, too. I think we should listen to Kristy."

"But what happens if, say, the library has another creative writing group?" Stacey pressed on. "Or Jessi's spring ballet class falls on a Wednesday?"

"What if neither of those things happen?" I countered. "Okay, sure, we'll have to deal with problems. We always have. If one of us wants to join another group, fine. If the times conflict, we'll mention our BSC commitment to the head of the group. They can be flexible, too."

No one spoke. Stacey looked deep in thought.

"Look," I went on, "I'm not expecting us to magically change. But if we do decide to re-form, we have to . . . reform! We each have to ask ourselves: Do we want this more than anything else? Are we ready to make the BSC our number one commitment again?"

"I am," Mallory and Jessi said at the same time.

Abby looked at Stacey. "Why are you being so negative? You told me you haven't been making enough money since the breakup."

"Well, that's true," Stacey admitted with a sigh, "I had to return most of the stuff I bought at the Steven E sale."

"You can't wear what you wore last fall?" Logan asked.

"You wouldn't understand." Stacey looked at him as if he'd suggested wearing iron chain mail. "I guess what I'm saying is, I feel torn. It would be great to have the BSC again, just the way it used to be. But we have to be like doctors. Treat the illness, not the symptoms. Don't forget how unhappy we were. Can we figure out the reasons? That's the only way to cure ourselves, if you know what I mean."

Claudia nodded. "No offense, Kristy, but it just wasn't fun anymore."

"I know that," I said. "I was the one who suggested we break up, remember? But we've been apart a long time. Sometimes that's the best thing for an illness, right? Rest and relaxation?"

"And lots of fluids," Abby added.

"I don't know about you guys," I went on, "but I feel much different now than I did a few weeks ago. The experience has affected me. Made me appreciate things I had been taking for granted. Like, what great sitters we are, and how well we work together."

"Friday night meetings, when we know there's no school the next day," Mary Anne volunteered.

"The looks on the kids' faces when we do

stuff with them on weekends," Shannon spoke up.

"Claudia's excellent catering," Logan added.

Stacey sighed. "The money."

"Face it," I said, "we're not happy about the breakup. Not to mention our clients aren't happy."

"I'm surprised they haven't run us out of town," Stacey remarked.

"Maybe we can do this," I continued. "Together. With everyone's input. Maybe we should go around the room and discuss what direction the club needs to go in — "

"Baby-sitting by fax," Logan suggested.

Shannon cracked up. "Use the Net."

"Virtual baby-sitting," Abby remarked.

"Be serious!" I thundered. "Uh . . . I mean, you know, when it's necessary."

Logan laughed. "Step right up to BSC, the Sequel — with Kristy Two, the new, improved, sensitive president."

Claudia was slowly sinking downward, anxiously popping Milk Duds into her mouth. "Tell me this is all a joke, please . . ."

"Claudia, *you* said that clients are calling all the time now," I said. "They wouldn't be, if they knew we were back to a schedule."

"Great, but I still don't understand how this

is going to help my grades. Besides . . ." Claudia cast a quick scowl at Mary Anne. "I'm just burned out from sitting."

"Tell the truth, Claudia," Mary Anne said in a tiny, trembling voice.

Claudia took a deep breath. "All right. I think some of us are, you know, uncompatible."

"*In-*," Shannon corrected her.

Claudia shrugged. "That, too."

"You don't like sitting with me," Mary Anne said.

"Well?" Claudia snapped. "The feeling goes both ways, doesn't it?"

Mary Anne nodded. Tears started streaming down her cheeks.

Logan put his arm around her and glared at Claudia.

But Claudia barrelled on. "Mary Anne, I just don't like the way you act when we're sitting together. You think I don't know as much as you. You don't ask me what we should do with the kids. You just assume you have the magic touch."

"You never told me you felt that way," Mary Anne said. "All you ever do is barge in and try to do things your way."

"Well, what else can I do?" Claudia asked.

"You're the one with the personality, Claudia. You're the one the kids like more. I feel so overshadowed when I'm with you. I can't be funny and creative. It's like, I'm the quiet, dull one. So I figure, okay, I'll make myself useful — organize the kids, keep them busy."

Claudia looked astonished. "Kids *adore* you, Mary Anne. You're such a good listener. You make them feel so good. I wish I could be like that."

"Really?"

"Really. And you honestly feel overshadowed by me?"

"Yup." Mary Anne wiped away a tear. "So I guess, like, we should . . . you know . . ."

"Communicate," said Jessi, Stacey, and I at the same time.

"Claudia, please don't think I look down on you," Mary Anne said softly. "I think you're a great sitter and a great person."

"You are, too," Claudia replied.

"I think I'm going to cry," Logan whimpered.

(Why oh why do we have a boy in this club?)

Mary Anne and Claudia both smiled and fell silent.

Finally Logan said, "Come on, you two, howzabout a big hug, huh?"

Claudia began pelting him with Milk Duds. "I vote we keep this club all girls!"

"Truce!" Logan cried, cowering.

"Food fight!" Abby called out.

"No!" Claudia shouted. "Not in my room!"

The door flew open and Janine poked her head in. She seemed perplexed to see us all. "Uh, excuse me, does this mean I need to buy another pair of earplugs?"

We all shut up and looked at each other.

"Well?" I said. "Does it?"

Claudia shrugged. "I'm still not sure, Kristy. Maybe. I admit, life has been pretty dreary since we broke up."

I looked around the room. "Okay, then. Here's what I want to know. Are we dedicated to a fresh start? Are we looking forward to the idea of three meetings a week? To putting our best energy into the work?"

"And into our friendships," Mary Anne added, sharing a smile with Claudia.

"I'm ready," Mallory spoke up.

"Me, too," Jessi agreed.

"Count me in," Abby said.

Mary Anne nodded, sniffling back a tear.

"Yup," said Logan.

"Fine with me," Shannon chimed in.

"No!" Stacey blurted out. "I mean, I just don't know. I want so badly to say yes. But I'm still thinking about what happened. I'm worried we'll slip back. Then what?"

I thought about that a moment. "Okay. Then how about a trial period? A probation time — say, we meet for one month and *then* decide if we'll continue for the rest of the year?''

"Good idea," Mary Anne said.

Around the room, heads were nodding.

"Okay," Stacey said. "If we do that, I think it's worth a try."

Claudia was still silent.

"Claud?" I said.

She shook her head. "If I flunk — "

"We'll help you," Stacey volunteered. "You'll have your BSC membership and quality tutoring, all in one."

"I'll be here for you," Janine said softly, still leaning against the door.

"Well . . . " Claudia murmured, a small smile inching across her face. "I guess . . ."

Time to strike. I took a deep breath. "I move, as former and possibly soon-to-be, or whatever, president of the Baby-sitters Club, that we reinstitutionalize . . . uh, reconstitute . . . no — "

"All in flavor say, 'Chips!' " Abby interrupted.

"CHIIIIIIPS!" yelled Claudia, Stacey, Mary Anne, Jessi, Mallory, Abby, Logan, Shannon, and I.

It was unanimous.

Claudia went to her closet to dig out a bag of tortilla chips.

Janine slunk out of the room.

Jessi and Mallory exchanged high-fives.

Mary Anne started bawling.

Abby put a tape in Claudia's boom box and began to dance.

Me? I felt pretty good.

We were together again. For at least another month.

Oh, well, I could take that. It was better than nothing.

Much better.

Dear Reader,

It's hard to believe, but *Kristy's Worst Idea* is the 100th book in the Baby-sitters Club series! When I first began writing the series, nobody, including me, had any idea that eventually over 100 books would be in the series. Incredibly, the month that this book was published marks the tenth anniversary of the publication of the first Baby-sitters Club book, *Kristy's Great Idea*, back in August 1986. So much has happened since then. The Baby-sitters Club has launched three other series, Baby-sitters Little Sister, the Baby-sitters Club Mysteries, and, most recently, The Kids in Ms. Colman's Class. The books have been translated into nineteen languages, including Chinese and Hebrew. There have been games, dolls, jewelry, clothing, a CD, and audiotapes. A true fan can also join the BSC fan club, watch the TV series, or rent the Baby-sitters Club movie. These have been ten great years and a hundred fun books. Maybe in the year 2005 we'll be celebrating the publication of book #200!

Happy reading,

Ann M. Martin

Ann M. Martin

About the Author

ANN MATTHEWS MARTIN was born on August 12, 1955. She grew up in Princeton, N.J., with her parents and her younger sister, Jane.

Although Ann used to be a teacher and then an editor of children's books, she's now a full-time writer. She gets the ideas for her books from many different places. Some are based on personal experiences. Others are based on childhood memories and feelings. Many are written about contemporary problems or events.

All of Ann's characters, even the members of the Baby-sitters Club, are made up. (So is Stoneybrook.) But many of her characters are based on real people. Sometimes Ann names her characters after people she knows, other times she chooses names she likes.

In addition to the Baby-sitters Club books, Ann Martin has written many other books for children. Her favorite is *Ten Kids, No Pets* because she loves big families and she loves animals. Her favorite Baby-sitters Club book is *Kristy's Big Day*. (By the way, Kristy is her favorite baby-sitter!)

Ann M. Martin now lives in New York. She has two cats, Gussie and Woody. Her hobbies are reading, needlework, and sewing — especially m clothes for children.

THE BABY-SITTERS CLUB

Notebook Pages

This Baby-sitters Club book belongs to _____Cayla_____.

I am ___5___ years old and in the _____ grade.

The name of my school is _____.

I got this BSC book from _____.

I started reading it on _____ and

finished reading it on _____.

The place where I read most of this book is _____.

My favorite part was when _____.

If I could change anything in the story, it might be the part when

_____.

My favorite character in the Baby-sitters Club is _____.

The BSC member I am most like is _____

_____.

_____by-sitters Club book it would be about ___

#100 Kristy's Worst Idea

Kristy thought that breaking up the BSC was a great idea . . . but it ended up being her worst idea ever! This is what I think about the BSC break-up: _____

_____

_____ . Without the BSC, parents have to call sitters individually. If I needed a sitter, the BSC member I would call first would be _____

_____ because _____

_____ . *Kristy's Worst Idea* is the hundredth book in the Baby-sitters Club series. Of the one hundred BSC books, I have read this many: _____

_____ . (And I want to read _____ more!) My favorite BSC book (so far) is _____

_____ because _____

_____ .

KRISTY'S

Playing softball with some of my favorite sitting charges.

A gab-fest

Me, age 3. Already on the go.

r mary anne!

My family keeps growing!

David michael, me, and
Louie — the best dog ever.

Illustrations by Angelo Tillery

Read all the books
about **Kristy**
in the Baby-sitters Club series
by Ann M. Martin

Look for #101

CLAUDIA KISHI,
MIDDLE SCHOOL DROPOUT

Mrs. Amer started things off by introducing herself to my parents. Everybody exchanged "Pleased to meet yous." Then Mr. Kingbridge (whom they've already met) began to talk about the trouble I'd been having, in all my subjects. He listed every single late homework assignment, every missed problem, and every failed pop quiz.

Humiliating? You bet.

But not surprising, to me or even to my parents. After all, they've watched me struggle all fall. They know it's been hard for me.

Then Mrs. Amer began to talk.

"Claudia," she said. "I don't know if you've thought about whether or not you want to go to college someday."

"College?" I asked. "Um —" To tell the truth, that seemed a long, long way off.

"Or even art school," Mrs. Amer continued.